"You deserve to be happy," Serena said.

"So do you." Why was she being so stubborn about this? Didn't she know how rare and precious love was? Hell, she couldn't have kissed him like that if she didn't still feel something for him.

Could she?

"Yes, I do deserve to be happy." She surprised him by agreeing. "And that's the problem. I'll never be happy married to a cop…"

Laura Iding loved reading as a child, and when she ran out of books she readily made up her own, completing a little detective mini-series when she was twelve. But, despite her aspirations for being an author, her parents insisted she look into a 'real' career, so the summer after she turned thirteen she volunteered as a Candy Striper and fell in love with nursing. Now, after twenty years of experience in trauma/critical care, she's thrilled to combine her career and her hobby into one—writing Medical Romances™ for Harlequin Mills & Boon®. Laura lives in the northern part of the United States and spends all her spare time with her two teenage kids (help!), a daughter and a son, and her husband. Enjoy!

We are proud to present

Laura Iding

An exciting new voice in Medical Romance™

EMERGENCY:
NURSE IN NEED

BY
LAURA IDING

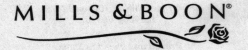

To my wonderful husband Scott.
Yes, honey, the check is in the mail!

First published in Great Britain 2004
Harlequin Mills & Boon Limited,
Eton House, 18-24 Paradise Road, Richmond, Surrey TW9 1SR

© Laura Iding 2004

ISBN 0 263 83930 3

Set in Times Roman 10½ on 12½ pt.
03-1004-40570

Printed and bound in Spain
by Litografia Rosés, S.A., Barcelona

CHAPTER ONE

A FULL moon hung ominously in the dark sky.

Serena Mitchell entered Milwaukee's Trinity Medical Center with a shiver and a deep sense of foreboding. A full moon was never a good sign. She should have checked her calendar before giving in to Dana's plea to cover her call shift for the night. But how could she turn Dana down, especially after hearing about Dana's mother's debilitating illness? Serena had started back to work in the trauma intensive care unit a few months ago, and was finding the old familiar routine was more difficult than she'd imagined. Not because of the patients themselves, they hadn't changed.

Because of the nightmares.

Maybe she should just quit. Home health nursing was an option. And then her patients would actually talk to her, rather than persist in hanging on the brink of a cliff, suspended between life and death.

Inside the trauma ICU she was greeted by a cacophony of noise and color. She took a deep breath and smoothed her damp palms along the sides of her scrubs. Everything would be fine. She'd gotten her life back on track. Returning to her old job proved it.

"Serena, I'm glad you're here." The charge nurse,

Tess Walker, glanced up from her clipboard. "The trauma room needs help."

Serena stifled a gasp and paled. "But I don't work the trauma room any more."

"You have trauma room experience, don't you?" Tess's voice rose in agitation.

"Well yes, but—"

"Look, we're having a bad night. They need your help. The trauma call just came in a minute ago. They've had their hands full down there all night. Later, you can report back up here." Tess turned her back, conversation over.

Serena wanted to argue, to flatly refuse to go. But when she glanced around, there wasn't an idle nurse in sight. Refusing her assignment in the trauma room would be the epitome of patient abandonment. No way was Serena willing to do that. And Tess was right about one thing—Serena was probably the only one here in the ICU with actual trauma room experience.

Experience that haunted her still.

She headed downstairs to the ground floor. Her rubber-soled shoes squeaked loudly on the shiny linoleum floor. Her trepidation deepened with every step. The thought of going back to the trauma room made her feel physically ill. She pushed back a wave of nausea with an effort.

Come on, Serena. You can do this.

She hesitated for a moment outside the doors, then forced herself to scan her name badge and walk inside.

The trauma room was busy, but not the worst she'd ever seen. Nothing looked horrifically different than the last time she'd been here, eighteen months ago. She was surprised to notice the two of the trauma bays stood empty.

"Hey, Serena!" Dr. Steve Anderson, the senior ER resident grinned at her. "Glad to have you back!"

"I'm not back, not really. Just helping out for a few minutes," she quickly qualified. Steve's cheerfulness was difficult to face. She forced herself to take a deep calming breath. "So what's going on? What are we waiting for?"

"Two victims with gunshot wounds to the chest." Steve gestured to the furthest trauma bay. "Why don't you take the right side over there?"

"What's the ETA?"

His answer was lost when the double doors slammed open and a bevy of paramedics burst into the emergency department wheeling a gurney between them. She could see a second patient not far behind. Shifting her feet slightly, she took her assigned place in the trauma bay.

Her heart pounded a deafening rhythm in her chest and she prayed she wouldn't disgrace herself by passing out cold. For a moment the room faded into a blur, the pounding in her ears growing louder, blanketing the noise around her. Serena brought the room into focus with a concentrated effort.

Controlled chaos prevailed. A throng of uniformed police officers filtered into the unit behind the gurneys and Serena experienced a horrible sense of *déjà vu*. The influx of cops reminded her too closely of the multitude of firefighters who'd invaded the trauma room when her brother Eric had been brought in. She closed her eyes against the painful memories.

Oh, God—Eric.

Someone grabbed her by the shoulders and shook her. Her head jerked up. Steve Anderson's face loomed over her.

"Snap out of it. We have work to do."

His stern tone made her blink—she hadn't been aware of Steve standing beside her. Then her gaze fell on the prone figure of her patient.

"Thirty-year-old white male police officer with multiple gunshot wounds, right chest and thigh." Another ED nurse shouted statistics above the din. "Two eighteen-gauge IVs of Ringer's lactate running wide open for hypovolemic shock. Intubated in the field. He needs six units of O-negative blood, stat."

Automatically assuming her role, Serena connected the patient to the monitor, intent on getting a baseline set of vital signs. She reached across the broad chest of the police officer, quickly placing EKG patches on the least bloody spots while trying to avoid the blood-soaked dressing over the wound on the right side. She concentrated on one task at a time, blocking out memories of Eric. She glanced up at the monitor and mentally noted a dangerously low blood pressure, before turning back to her patient.

She caught a glimpse of the officer's face and drew

a harsh breath. Once again, the room spun wildly. Her fingers turned numb as she fumbled with the blood-pressure tubing. She grabbed the gurney for support.

Not again—please, not again...

Sweat popped out on her forehead. Serena blinked to bring his face back into focus, thinking that there must be some sort of mistake. But when her vision cleared she couldn't deny the truth. Despite the liberal splattering of blood, she recognized her patient.

Grant Sullivan.

The man she once promised to marry.

Another nurse had already hung several units of blood on the rapid infuser on the opposite side of the bed. Steve barked out orders. "This guy needs a chest tube. Serena, what the hell are you doing? We need that blood, *stat!*"

Serena jerked her gaze away from Grant's face and grabbed two units of O-negative blood. Years of deeply imbedded training took over. She announced the vital signs for everyone's benefit. "Heart rate 160, blood pressure 70 over 30, core temp 96 degrees. He's still in shock."

Steve didn't waste any more time. "Hang four more units of blood on the rapid infuser. He needs a chest tube." As he spoke he prepared the right side of Grant's chest with antimicrobial solution.

Struggling to suppress her horror, Serena's nightmare became grim reality. Functioning solely on autopilot, she hung more units of blood onto the tubing of the rapid infuser. Somehow, even with high-tech machinery, she couldn't seem to get the lifesaving fluid into him fast enough.

Don't die, Grant. Damn it, don't you dare die on me!

Serena checked his blood pressure again, her heart sinking when she realized they hadn't made much headway. The nurse on the other side of the bed also hung more blood. Heaven knew, Grant's vital organs needed what little blood he had left in his system.

Grant flinched beneath her hands when Steve placed the chest tube. She swallowed a wave of nausea even as she helped to connect the tubing. Aghast, they both stared as bright red blood poured from Grant's lung.

"Dammit!" Steve yelled to a nurse across the room. "Get me a CT surgery consult—*now*! This guy needs the OR."

He left the dressing of the chest tube site to Serena but her fingers didn't readily co-operate as she tried to tape the gauze in place. The chief resident of cardiothoracic surgery walked over from the other side of the trauma bay. Serena was vaguely aware of the activity surrounding the second patient that had been brought in with Grant.

"What do you have?"

"Gunshot wound to the chest and thigh, profuse bleeding and hypovolemic shock. He needs the OR, stat."

"Yeah? Well, so does the guy over there." He jerked a thumb in the general direction of the second patient. Then the chief resident noticed the large pool of blood pouring through Grant's chest tube. He sighed. "Hell. We'll call in a second team and take both of them at the same time."

One of the police officers not in uniform stepped directly into the path of the surgeon. Large and barrel-chested, the cop wore a loud plaid sports jacket that looked to be two sizes too small. In spite of his receding hairline and the wad of gum he chewed noisily between his teeth, he was obviously the senior officer in charge.

"What did you say? You're taking both of them at the same time?" At the physician's confirming nod, the group of police officers subtly stepped forward in wordless support of their leader. "I'm Captain Reichert, and I insist you take Detective Sullivan first. The other guy is the perp who shot him. No point in saving him when he's going to do time for attempted murder."

The surgeon didn't back down, despite the threatening tone of the police captain's voice, possessing more than enough arrogance of his own. "My job is to save lives. You're in my way."

"Take Detective Sullivan first."

The surgeon stepped forward as if to push past the officers, but the group of uniformed men didn't budge. The surgeon tried again. "I can't judge whose life is more important, they're all important to me. You have my word that we'll do everything possible to save your cop's life. But I'm telling you, we're operating on both patients at the same time.''

For a moment Serena wondered if a fight would break out in the middle of the trauma room. With a scathing look, the thick-set police captain eventually backed down. He gave one last parting shot. ''We already lost one officer tonight. I promise you, my chief will personally call your CEO if Sullivan dies and the perp lives.''

After the captain had delivered that dire warning, the rest of the officers moved out of the way. Serena breathed a small sigh of relief. There'd been more than enough bloodshed for one night.

Steve didn't have to tell Serena to give more blood—she automatically continued to hang one unit after another. Grabbing Steve's arm, she asked, ''How bad is the thigh wound? Could his femoral artery be nicked?''

''Possibly. Get me a vascular tray.''

Anticipating his request, Serena had it open and ready to go.

''Nice job, Rena.'' They fell into an old familiar routine as he deftly arranged the instruments.

Removing the paramedics' dressing on Grant's thigh, she exposed the injured area.

''This is the exit wound.'' Blood gushed and Serena quickly covered the wound with a pile of gauze, placing both her hands over the area and bearing down with all her strength. Grant flinched. She bit her lip. The pain he subconsciously felt must be agonizing.

She felt the heavy stare of each police officer in the trauma bay as they suspiciously gauged her every move. They couldn't know that hurting Grant was the furthest thing from her mind. Once she'd loved him with her whole heart. But that had been in the past. A memory that needed to stay dead and buried so that she could finish her job.

"OK, let me see."

Serena maintained pressure above the wound with one hand, removing the gauze with the other. Blood swelled, obscuring his view. She swiped it out of the way with another piece of gauze.

"There. I found it." Working quickly, he clamped the artery and sutured up the tear. Serena didn't let up on the pressure, although her arms trembled and ached from the effort.

"You're right, this is the exit wound. Strange, considering the wound in his chest is from the opposite angle. At least there's no bullet in this wound." Steve nodded to Serena and she backed off on the pressure. Elbowing the light out of the way, he ripped off his bloody gloves. "That's good enough until he gets to the OR."

Serena covered the wound with more sterile gauze before refastening the mast pants. Then hung two more units of blood.

"He looks like he's stabilizing, although that pressure isn't going to sustain him for long." Steve scowled, peering through the crowd. ''Where the hell are those surgical teams?''

Serena knew she should do a quick assessment, but her mind went blank. For the life of her she couldn't remember what to do first. The image of her brother's soot-blackened face swam in front of her eyes. She shook her head forcefully, willing the haunting memories away.

Eric was gone, but Grant was here and he needed her expertise, inadequate though it might be.

''Come on, think.'' Now that she had time, she couldn't string two coherent thoughts together. There was an intangible pressure from the bevy of cops that watched her. Finally, she began a neurologic assessment. A mistake, because when she looked down at Grant's blood-streaked face her eyes burned with unshed tears.

Why hadn't he listened to her? She'd warned him that something like this would happen, but had he cared? No, he'd chosen life as a cop over her love. Once a hero, always a hero. And if Grant had his way, damn his stubborn male pride, he'd *die* a hero.

Not tonight, dammit. He's not going to die tonight!

Sniffling, she blinked the wetness from her eyes and forced herself to listen to Grant's heart and lungs. She tried to look at him like any other patient, but it wasn't easy. Finally, the cardiothoracic team surrounded the bedside just as she finished her abdominal exam.

''OK, let's move.''

Within moments they had the monitors disconnected and the surgical team took over, wheeling
Grant, with the second victim right behind him,
through the trauma bay to the elevator that would
carry them to the lower-level operating suites. Serena
walked alongside his gurney. She was only allowed
as far as the perimeter of the OR suite, then could
only stand and watch as they settled him on the OR
table, draping him from view. His life was no longer
in the hands of the trauma team, but in those of the
talented cardiothoracic surgeons.

She stared in numb exhaustion as the OR doors
closed right in front of her face. A sob of despair rose
from her throat. She'd thought she'd gotten her life
back on track but coming face to face with Grant had
only reaffirmed the opposite. How was it possible
she'd never really gotten over him?

Dear God, please let him live…

CHAPTER TWO

HER shift was far from over. The fact that Grant hadn't died beneath her hands only brought a small measure of relief. Grant wasn't out of danger yet. Serena wanted nothing more than to fall face first onto a cot in the nurses' lounge, but there was too much work to be done.

The job of escorting the dozen or so cops milling around the ICU to the waiting room fell to her. She briefly instructed them to wait there while Detective Grant Sullivan was in surgery. After getting them settled with a fresh pot of coffee, Serena explained that once Grant returned, she or another nurse would call them in to see him.

Most of the time the hospital only allowed immediate family members to visit, but in this case the officers would be allowed in two at a time in rotation. Serena was about to leave when the captain stopped her with a hand on her arm.

"I'm Captain Reichert, ma'am. We need to be informed about the perp's condition." He frowned and shifted the wad of gum to the other side of his mouth. "Once out of surgery, we'll need to post a guard on him twenty-four seven."

Serena nodded, knowing he was only explaining

standard operating procedure. Seeing a guard posted outside a patient's room wasn't anything new, even while the prisoner was in Intensive Care and generally too sick to be considered a threat. She didn't know much about the other patient, her energy had been focused on Grant. But from what she'd briefly over-heard, this guy had most likely shot two police offi-cers, leaving one of them dead. No question, he'd be in police custody from now on.

"I understand. What was his name again? I'll give the information to the nurses." Serena had been far too busy taking care of Grant to spare a second thought to the victim that had arrived simultaneously with him.

"Jason Roth." The captain nervously bobbed his head once more, clearly uncomfortable with the hos-pital atmosphere. She didn't blame him. This type of incident only reaffirmed your own mortality, espe-cially when involved in such a dangerous profession.

Steve gave Serena the OK to head back to the trauma ICU. She needed to update the charge nurse on the status of the two post-surgical patients and the fact that one of them would be under police guard.

Tess Walker took the news in her stride and iden-tified their last two empty rooms, which were side by side for the pending arrivals. She instructed Serena to stay in the trauma ICU to help with the activity there while they waited for information from the operating room. Serena pitched in, assisting her co-workers.

Oddly enough, the critical care setting was a relief

after her experience in the trauma room. Yet Serena couldn't stop thinking about Grant. She tried not to dwell on the fact that he might not make it. Eric, her brother, had been strong and healthy, too, when he'd died in the trauma room but the human body was designed to withstand only so much punishment. Two bullets ripping through arteries and vital organs, causing severe blood loss, tended to push the limit.

How like Grant not to have his body armor on. He'd always acted as if he were invincible. She knew differently. The vision of him lying beneath her hands, bleeding profusely, hovered in her mind's eye throughout the next hour.

The operating room called to report that Jason Roth would be coming out shortly. Serena walked down the hall to the ICU waiting room to give Captain Reichert the news. Understandably, he was less than thrilled with the situation.

"Why in the hell is Roth's surgery over already? How's Sullivan doing?" The captain paced back and forth in the small space of the waiting room, one hand absently rubbing the center of his chest as his jaw clenched hard on the wad of gum still in his teeth.

Serena noticed his gesture, wondering if the grouchy captain had a history of heart problems or if he just suffered from chronic heartburn. She sympathized with his frustration, but could only shake her head. "I don't know, we haven't heard anything about Detective Sullivan yet."

"Dammit, I don't like this. I don't like it at all."

Serena nodded. She didn't much like the situation either. Time seemed to stand still as Grant's life hung in the balance. She glanced around the room full of police officers and another thought struck her. "Have you been in contact with Detective Sullivan's family? He has a sister, Cheryl, who lives in Denver."

The captain nodded and smoothed a hand over his bald spot. If he wondered how Serena knew about Grant's sister, he didn't let on. "Yeah, she's on her way. I'd like to give her good news when she gets here."

Serena silently agreed. Cops stood by each other in times like this, a true brotherhood. But Grant and Cheryl were close, too, despite the miles between them. Their parents had died in a car crash a few years previously, and they only had each other now. Cheryl must be a basket case, wondering what she'd find when she finally arrived. "Will you call me when she gets here?"

Captain Reichert frowned and nodded. Serena returned to the ICU, glancing at her watch to note she still had a good four hours until the end of her shift.

She passed the time helping to get Jason settled in after his surgery. Serena was dismayed to find out that he was barely fifteen. She felt sick at the thought of a teenager running around the streets with a gun. He'd suffered a gunshot wound to his chest, presumably put there by Grant. Jason was lucky. Youth was on his side. He'd most likely recover without any problems.

A police officer from the waiting room took up residence as a guard outside the doorway to Jason's room.

One of the operating room aides approached Serena after she came out of Jason's room. He thrust two plastic bags of blood-soaked clothing at Serena. "We took these off the two trauma victims. This bag is from the suspect, Jason Roth. The cops were looking for his things to keep as evidence. This other one belongs to the cop. He has a wallet in there so you'd better call Security to have it locked up in the safe."

Serena accepted the burden with a grimace. "Thanks. I'll take care of them."

She set Grant's things at his empty bedside and took the bag containing Jason's bloody clothes to the captain in the waiting room. He was thrilled with her dubious gift, immediately sending one of his men back down to the station with the evidence. When Serena returned to the unit, she did as suggested and called Security to pick up Grant's wallet.

The guard arrived a few minutes later. Serena opened Grant's wallet to count the money with the security guard as a witness. Together they counted out the cash and placed the money in an envelope before sealing it shut. As she closed his wallet, Serena's gaze noted a seemingly new picture of a beautiful brunette laughing into the camera.

A shaft of jealousy pierced her heart. Snapping the wallet closed, she handed it over to the security guard along with the cash. The bloodied and ripped clothing she saved for the police, figuring they might need them for evidence as well.

The image of the pretty brunette wouldn't go away. Grant's personal life was none of her business. She knew herself well enough to know that she couldn't handle the risks of his career. Not after the way she'd lost her brother. So she'd returned Grant's ring, ending their relationship. She hadn't seen him in eighteen months. If he'd replaced her with the brunette, more power to him. He deserved to be happy.

Cool logic, though, didn't ease the knot of resentment in her stomach. Why hadn't Grant loved her enough to quit? Or at least to transfer into something that might not be as dangerous. Serena put a hand over her lower abdomen, as if to ease the ache there.

She wondered if the brunette would show up at the hospital once she heard the news of Grant's injury. Serena didn't know if she could tolerate chatting with her replacement face to face, comparing notes. Maybe she'd give Grant to another nurse.

Or, then again, maybe not. Her shift was almost over. She wanted to see this thing through. Another painstaking hour passed before they heard word about Grant. Finally the OR nurse called into the unit to announce that their patient would be out of surgery in fifteen minutes.

Serena used that time to make sure everything was ready in his room, then informed the captain of the news. Cheryl still hadn't arrived yet, but the captain was temporarily satisfied to hear that his detective had survived the surgery.

Grant's arrival from the operating room was accomplished with fanfare. Clearly, his condition was far less stable than Jason Roth's. Serena barely had time to catch her breath. The room was packed with a variety of medical personnel, many of whom shouted orders.

She and the other nurses quickly connected the monitoring equipment. Both the cardiothoracic surgeon and the anesthesiologist remained at the bedside for a long time, making sure their patient wouldn't require another trip to the operating room. Serena didn't care if she bordered on breaking ethical rules by keeping Grant as her patient. What was the harm? They weren't engaged any more. And no one would care about him more than she would. She simply couldn't walk away.

The OR staff had cleaned away the worst of the blood. One large gauze dressing covered half his chest and another encircled his thigh. His familiar, finely sculpted body lay completely still underneath the various tubes and machinery. At least his vital signs were stable. At this point Serena wouldn't ask for anything more than that.

"Does this guy have family here?" The cardiothoracic surgeon commanded Serena's attention. "I'm not talking to that horde of cops out there."

Serena didn't bother to point out that those cops probably meant more to Grant than anyone else. Certainly, they'd meant more to him than she had. "He has a sister on her way from Denver. Why don't you fill me in on what you did during surgery so I can pass that information along to her? All the cops need to know is that he's stable. I can always page you when his sister arrives.''

''Fine.'' He proceeded to do just that and Serena tried not to show any reaction as he described in detail just how tenuous the surgical procedure had been. Apparently they had come close to losing Grant on the table, needing to give him large doses of medication and blood products to bring him back. Grant had lost an entire lobe of his lung as well as tearing the muscle and nicking the artery in his right thigh.

Serena knew that Grant was lucky to have escaped with his life, but she wondered how he'd react to the extent of his injuries. Would the limitations from the gunshot wounds prevent him from remaining a cop? She despised herself for the surge of hope. With a shake of her head, she reminded herself that there was already a woman in his life. Even if Serena had wanted to give their relationship another try, which she didn't, the love they'd once shared was gone. Truthfully, Serena didn't think she'd ever risk loving anyone again. Besides, Grant's determination was legendary. If there was a way to get back on the job, he'd find it.

Serena was too busy to leave Grant's bedside, so she had one of the other nurses call Captain Reichert in from the waiting room. Keeping a close eye on Grant's pulse and blood pressure, she finished up the rest of her paperwork.

"Ma'am?" Captain Reichert stood outside the doorway of Grant's room, looking distinctly uncomfortable in the face of medical high technology. Sweat beaded his brow, and his ruddy complexion deepened.

"Hello." Serena gave him an encouraging smile. "Well, so far, so good. The surgery took longer than anticipated, but his vital signs are stable. In fact, I'm easing off on some of the medication they had him on during the operation."

Captain Reichert bravely took a few steps into the room, scowling as he looked at the prone figure in the bed. "Will he wake up?"

"I'm sure he will once the anesthesia wears off. His body needs time to recover from the dual assaults of the trauma and subsequent surgery." Serena did her best to reassure him. "The next twenty-four hours are critical, but so far he's holding his own. Has Cheryl arrived yet?"

The captain chewed his gum hard, with a grinding motion of his jaw. "She called from the airport, some delay with her connecting flight. I told her he's out of surgery."

"Good. The surgeon, Dr. Hardy, will want to know when she's here."

"I remember." Captain Reichert's bloodshot gaze narrowed and he shifted the wad of gum to the other side of his mouth. "I'd like to see him, too. I have an officer standing by to take the evidence down to the station."

Serena raised an eyebrow. "Evidence?"

"The bullet they dug out of Sullivan's chest." He glanced towards the room next to Grant, where one of his men sat in a chair, guarding Jason. "We need it to prove that Roth shot and killed one officer and mortally wounded another." The captain sounded particularly pleased by the notion of charging Jason Roth for murder.

Not that she could blame him. The thought of locking up Grant's assailant gave her satisfaction, too. The captain stayed for a few minutes, then returned to the waiting room.

Serena brought her gaze back to Grant, lying motionless beneath the monitoring equipment. She spoke to him, like she did all her patients.

"Grant? It's me, Serena. You're in the ICU but you're doing fine. Just relax and let us take care of you." She laid her hand on his forehead, resisting the ridiculous urge to lean down and press her lips there. Once she'd known every dimple, every inch of Grant's body better than her own. Her fingertips tingled from the memory of his touch. She wondered how much he'd changed in the months since they'd parted ways.

He wasn't hers to care about on a personal level. Serena stepped back from the bedside to give the next two cops that hovered outside the doorway room to enter. They spoke briefly to the guard outside Jason's room, and she overheard them say something about making sure the DA tried the kid as an adult.

She frowned. They probably had saved Jason's life, only to have him tried for murder. As a nurse she should remain nonjudgmental, yet she silently sided with the captain on this one. In her opinion, Grant should have been taken into surgery first.

Fatigue overpowered the leftover adrenaline rush. The clock told her she had barely an hour of her shift yet to go. Serena pried her eyes open, hoping she'd stay awake that long.

She kept herself busy in the time remaining, but just as she was about to leave the unit she searched for Tess, the charge nurse. After a few moments reviewing the schedule, Serena signed up to work both Saturday and Sunday night shifts, covering the rest of the weekend. She didn't let on that her only reason for doing so was to keep a close eye on Grant. Serena told herself that this wasn't anything personal, she'd care about her other friends the same way.

But deep down she suspected the real reason was much more complicated than that.

A sweetly reassuring voice pulled him from the deep recesses of consciousness. But then pain hit. Mind-numbing, exploding pain covering every inch of his body. He savored the cool, gentle touch of a hand on his forehead for bare seconds before the cresting pain took control. Unable to fight, he slipped back into blessed oblivion.

*   *   *

Bone weary, Serena squinted through the bright morning sunlight that shone through the windows as she trudged upstairs to the second floor of her apartment building. Working the graveyard shift was tough. Luckily, the early summer day was cool, so she'd have no problem sleeping in her non-air-conditioned apartment. She couldn't wait to reach her bed. But a flash of a young boy dashing past the stairs startled her.

"Rico?" Going on instinct, she took the stairs two at a time. She had just enough time to see the twelve-year-old dark-haired boy slipping into the apartment directly across from hers.

She marched up to the Gonzales apartment and banged her fist on his door. "Rico, open up. It's me, Serena."

After a prolonged pause the door opened a crack, although he didn't remove the safety chain. She hunkered down so she could peer through the slit to look directly into Rico's wide, wary eyes.

"Did you just get home?" It was barely eight on a Saturday morning.

He shrugged, eyes downcast.

"Is Marta at work?"

This time he slowly nodded.

"You're supposed to stay inside when your sister is working, aren't you?"

He nodded again, but the way he avoided her gaze told her he hadn't followed the rules. Again. She sighed. The boy was home alone after school and all day on the weekends while Marta worked two jobs in an effort to put food on the table. Seven years younger than Serena, Marta was only twenty-one, young to be cast in the role as Rico's guardian. Serena had always considered Rico to be a fairly responsible kid. Now she wasn't so sure.

"Rico." She tried again to reach him. He wasn't exactly her problem but over the past year she'd gotten to know Rico and Marta fairly well. Where had he been? Surely he couldn't have been out all night? "Would you like to come over to my place for a while? Keep me company?"

The seconds stretched. She held her breath. In the end he wordlessly shook his head again and quietly shut the door between them.

CHAPTER THREE

SERENA awoke momentarily disoriented by the late evening light slanting through her bedroom window. After a few minutes, the events from last night came flooding back.

Grant had been shot. Twice. In the line of duty.

Serena peered at the clock, pushing a hand through her mass of tangled hair. In five hours she needed to be back at Trinity for her next shift. How had Grant fared during the past ten hours? Had his condition stabilized?

Trudging to the bathroom, Serena had to fight the urge to call the unit to check up on him. She didn't need to get emotionally involved, especially when he'd clearly moved on to someone else. Still, her chest ached as if he'd held her close just yesterday, rather than eighteen months ago.

Breaking their engagement had been the right thing to do. If they'd have stayed together, Serena was sure she'd have made Grant's life miserable, worrying over every moment he was out on the street. Grant needed someone to support him, not someone who would fall apart at every domestic abuse call broadcast over the scanner.

Many spouses listened to the police scanner while

their loved ones were working. Serena simply couldn't understand it. Why would you want to hear the bad news over the radio? Maybe her career in the trauma room had trained her to always think the worst, because her imagination was way too vivid to calmly listen to each succinct detail about the types of calls the cops responded to.

As she dressed in a clean pair of scrubs, Serena overheard a commotion outside her door. Remembering her altercation with Rico that morning, she poked her head outside.

"Marta?"

The pretty young Hispanic woman from across the hall banged her fist against the wall in frustration.

"What is it? Where's Rico?"

"That's just it. *Dios*, I don't know where he's gone." The younger woman's eyes filled with tears. "He's been leaving without telling me where he's going. I don't know what to do any more, Serena."

A chill slithered down her spine as Serena recalled the boy's antics earlier that morning. "Calm down. Is he hanging around with his school friends?"

Marta shook her head. "No, no. I've already called. No one admits to seeing him."

Serena's stomach sank quicker than lead. "OK, then maybe we should call the police. He's a minor. They'll look for him and bring him home." Even as she voiced the words, Marta's big brown eyes widened in horror.

"No. *Esta loco?* They'll call Social Services and take him away from me. No police. I will find him."

Serena glanced at her watch with a sigh. She only had a few hours before she needed to report in. "We'll both go and search for him. But we'll meet back here in two hours, because I have to work tonight."

With a relieved smile, Marta nodded. "Okay."

While valiant, their efforts proved to be useless. She and Marta split up the search area to cover more ground. But although Serena drove slowly through the winding streets around Rico's school, the park where most of the kids hung out and all the territory in between, she came up empty.

Come on, Rico. Where are you?

She returned to the apartment building at the designated time. Marta arrived a few minutes later. When she saw that Serena's car was empty, her features clouded over again.

Serena steeled herself against a flash of sympathy. "Call the police, Marta. Please."

Stubbornly, the young woman shook her head. Serena didn't want to force the issue, but she worried that if Marta didn't make the call first, the police would be contacting her instead. Neither option boded well for the young woman desperate to provide a home for her young brother.

When the time came that she needed to leave for work, Serena hated the thought of leaving Marta alone. She convinced Marta to call her at Trinity the moment she'd heard from Rico. The fate of the young boy gnawed at her during the short drive in to the hospital.

Once in the unit, she headed straight to the assignment board to write her name next to Grant's. Her co-workers didn't argue since they knew she'd admitted him the night before. If they remembered that she had once been engaged to a cop named Grant Sullivan, they didn't mention it.

Except for her close friend, Dana. Chronically late, Dana Whitney had arrived long after the assignments had been doled out. Serena dodged the questioning looks Dana repeatedly sent in her direction. Luckily, the busyness of their respective patients prevented any small talk.

Serena took a report from the second shift nurse, a petite little blonde named Emma. They both entered Grant's room to look over his chart. Serena listened to Emma with one ear, but was troubled by the fact that Grant showed no sign of waking up. The effects of the anesthesia should have worn off by now.

After a few minutes, she thought Grant's eyelids fluttered, as if he might be regaining consciousness.

"Grant?" Serena smoothed his sandy brown hair away from his forehead in a comforting gesture that was an innate part of her nursing care. Maybe her fingers lingered on his face longer than usual. "It's Serena again. I'm your nurse for the night."

Emma informed Serena that Cheryl was waiting in a small quiet room just outside the unit. Serena acknowledged the information with a nod but then her gaze landed on Jason. She jerked her chin in his direction.

"Hey, Em. How's the guy next door doing?"

Emma raised her eyebrow at Serena's blatant curiosity. "Actually, he's doing great. He woke up this evening and I think they're going to try to extubate him in the morning." She shook her head with a tired smile. "The cops can't wait. They have a lot of questions for that boy."

"I bet." Questions that he couldn't answer with a breathing tube stuck in his throat. Serena sighed and turned her attention back to Grant. "Thanks for the info. See you tomorrow."

Serena went about her duties, trying to ignore how helpless Grant looked wearing nothing but a hospital gown. Boy, he'd really hate knowing that once he awoke. She checked his vital signs and hung an antibiotic. She also gave him another shot of morphine, knowing that the small incremental doses wouldn't be enough to keep him from regaining consciousness. Hopefully the medication at least took the edge off his pain.

When she needed to check his thigh dressing, her fingers trembled a bit as she lifted his gown just high enough to see the edge of the incision. Her objectivity vanished, making her doubt the wisdom of her decision to take care of Grant as his nurse. When he awoke, would he resent the fact that she was here, seeing him at his most vulnerable?

''Serena?'' one of her peers called from the nurses' station.

''Yes?'' She applied a new dressing and walked to the open doorway. The police officer seated in the chair outside Jason's room gave her a polite greeting. Serena flashed a small smile in return.

''Your patient's sister, Cheryl, is calling from the quiet room. She wants to know if she can come back in to see him.''

''Of course. Send her in.'' Serena quickly returned to Grant's bedside. She straightened the sheet covering him, then leaned over his bed. ''Hey, Grant. Your sister is here to see you. She came all the way from Colorado, so maybe you can try to open your eyes for her.''

Serena paused for a moment, searching for any kind of response. For a moment she thought his hand moved so she reached down to clasp it in hers. Longing hit hard and her fingers tightened imperceptibly at the familiar grip.

''Well, don't worry. I don't think she's going anywhere yet. We'll just have to wait until you're good and ready to wake up, won't we?'' It was a rhetorical question, but that's what happened when you carried on a one-sided conversation. Serena gave Grant's hand a reassuring squeeze and wished he'd wake up.

''Hi. The nurse said I could come in.''

Serena turned and mentally braced herself for the worst. She wondered if Grant had told his sister the reason they'd called off their engagement. She forced a smile. "Hello, Cheryl. How are you?"

"Serena?" Surprised and wary, Cheryl stepped through the doorway. "I didn't expect to find you here."

"I'm taking care of Grant."

"So I see." She stood on the opposite side of his bed, staring at him for a long time, her eyes slowly filling with despair. "What's wrong with him? Why hasn't he woken up yet?"

"Shh. It's OK." Serena wrapped her arms around Cheryl's shoulders, providing what little comfort she could offer. "I know how hard it is to believe, but he's doing just fine."

Cheryl's expression mirrored her doubt. "How can you tell? That he's doing better, I mean?"

"There's a number of things. I just turned off his blood-pressure medicine because he doesn't need it any more. His electrolytes are returning to normal and his blood count is stable. I know these sound like little things, but they're all signs he's getting better."

"I hope so." Cheryl sniffed and blinked back her tears. "How come you're taking care of him, Serena?"

"Because I care." She didn't know how to make Cheryl believe her. "I knew that getting married would have been the wrong thing for us, but you need to know, Cheryl, I didn't stop caring about Grant."

Cheryl was quiet for a moment, then dredged up a

tremulous smile. "I'm glad you're here. I appreciate a friendly face."

"Me, too." Serena glanced back down at Grant and put a hand on his arm. "Just be patient. Hopefully he'll wake up soon."

The voice called again, this time clearer than before. He thought the melodious voice asked him to wake up and he tried to put out a hand to keep her talking. The pain still throbbed with every beat of his pulse but, instead of his entire body being engulfed in the sensation, he thought it was centered now on his chest and leg. Grant felt the familiar, soothing touch on his hand and concentrated on the voice. The voice could save him from the dark pain but why couldn't he open his eyes? The harder he tried to fight, the worse the pain became until he slid down once more into the well of blackness.

"I'm going to lie down in the quiet room," Cheryl informed Serena. "I'm beat. I don't know how you nurses manage to stay up all night. You'll call me if anything changes, won't you?"

"Of course." Serena nodded.

Cheryl hesitated in the doorway. "That boy in the next room, the one with the police officer sitting outside his door. He's the one who shot Grant, isn't he?"

Serena hesitated, then answered honestly. "Yes, the police think so. They were both brought in last night from the crime scene."

Cheryl frowned. "I'm not sure I like him right next door. But, then, I don't think I like him in the same hospital, or even the same city."

"I know what you mean." Serena shrugged. "I'm sorry. Most of our ICU beds were full at the time, so we didn't have many options."

Cheryl sighed and shook her head, her gaze drifting back to Jason. "He looks so young, barely old enough to drive. It sure makes you wonder, doesn't it?" Without waiting for an answer, Cheryl bid her good-night.

Serena looked back at Grant and speculated, not for the first time, about what had happened last night. One cop dead, another mortally wounded—she could almost imagine the sound of gunfire exploding through the silence of the night. Serena knew Grant well enough to know that he wasn't reckless by nature. But he didn't back down from a fight either. That was one of the things she loved about him, and the characteristic she dreaded the most.

Why had he been on the scene so late last night? Detectives didn't usually work such long hours. He wasn't a beat cop any more. Why couldn't someone else have responded instead?

She sighed. Detective or not, Grant was a cop. Nothing would change that fact. So what had been the cause of such needless death? A drug deal gone bad? An argument over gang turf? Serena had worked long enough in critical care to know that not only did the seedy side of life exist, those who lived it were constantly in battle over some stupid thing or another. She couldn't imagine what satisfaction Grant gained from fighting on the losing side of that war.

Leaving people like her to piece the casualties back together again. As far as she was concerned, heroes were vastly overrated. They couldn't keep you company in the darkest hours of the night because they were only human. And those who courted death too often eventually paid the price.

Her brother Eric had been the same. He hadn't listened to her concerns either.

Serena pushed herself away from Grant's bed and busied herself with the other small tasks that needed to be done. Since her brother's death, she'd understood her own limitations. And had learned to live with them. She'd experienced too many losses to take life for granted. All she wanted was to lead a normal life, maybe even someday have a family. That wasn't too much to ask, was it? But watching Grant lying in a hospital bed and fighting for his life reopened old wounds, making them ooze.

"Rena?" Dana poked her head into Grant's room. "There's a phone call for you. Marta, I think she said."

Eager for the distraction, Serena dashed to the phone. "Marta? You found him?"

"He just came home." The earlier fear in Marta's voice was now punctuated with barely suppressed anger. "Can you believe it? He strolls in at two in the morning, as if nothing is wrong."

Serena winced. Ouch. "Where was he?"

"I don't know." Marta's tone reflected her frustration. "He's not telling."

The sinking feeling in her stomach intensified. Serena feared Rico was up to no good. There had been lots of rumors about gangs moving into the outskirts of the city. Into the park located just down the street from the school. "Look, I'll talk to him tomorrow. Right now, I need to get back to work."

"OK. *Gracias*, Serena."

Lost in thought, Serena returned to Grant's room where she found Dana waiting for her. She sighed. "Hi, Dana."

Her friend raised an eyebrow at her. "Do you need any help?"

Serena gave up trying to dodge the questions she knew were coming. Throwing a lopsided smile at her friend, she nodded. "Sure, help me turn him."

"So what gives?" Dana asked as they eased the muscular bulk of Grant over to his left side. Serena propped a pillow behind his back to keep him there. "I almost fell over when I saw your name next to Grant's on the assignment board. Are you trying to torture yourself over past mistakes? I practically had to twist your arm to get you to cover for me last night."

"How is your mother, by the way? Is she doing any better?" Serena carefully lifted Grant's right arm, placing another pillow beneath it, to keep the weight off his chest incision.

For a moment a dark cloud settled over Dana's delicate facial features. "Actually, she's not tolerating the chemotherapy treatments very well." Dana hesitated, then confided, "I'm thinking of asking for some time off to take care of her full time."

Serena threw her friend a startled glance. "I'm sorry. Is there anything I can do to help? I could check on her between shifts."

Dana shook her head. "It's sweet of you to offer, but I think I can handle it for now. But let's get back to the subject at hand."

"I won't lie to you, Dana. Last night they pulled me down to the trauma room." Serena blew her wispy bangs off her forehead, sweating from the exertion of moving Grant. "I helped resuscitate him while the place swarmed with cops."

Dana winced, familiar with the circumstances surrounding Eric's death. "I'm sorry that you had to relive those painful memories. But maybe it's for the better. Now that you've made it past the first hurdle, you might consider applying for your old job."

"I'm not going back," Serena warned, giving Grant another dose of morphine. Prior to working in the ICU she'd worked the trauma room. "But I couldn't leave him either. Not without seeing this through. I won't be satisfied until he's up on his feet."

Dana sighed, glancing down at Grant. "I wish you'd reconsider. Avoiding the past isn't the same thing as dealing with it. Grant isn't your brother. He'll make it. He's made it this far, hasn't he?''

Serena narrowed her gaze. "Eric took all the necessary precautions, and nothing could save him. Grant wasn't even wearing body armor. By rights, he should already be dead.''

"So now you're mad because he didn't die?" Dana threw up her hands in defeat. "You're not making any sense, Serena.''

"I suppose not." Serena didn't understand the bitter emotion that threatened to choke her. "I don't know what's wrong with me. I guess I'm still angry that Grant didn't love me enough to consider a less dangerous position.''

"But you're here, taking care of him.''

"Yeah. I guess." Dana was right, no point in arguing that one.

Dana left to take care of her own patients. Serena stared down at Grant for a long moment then she reluctantly left the bedside to tend to her second patient. The woman was an elderly woman who had come down with pneumonia after undergoing a hip replacement. Luckily, the woman's ventilator settings indicated she was getting stronger. They were slowly but surely weaning her from the vent. Serena estimated that she'd be out of Intensive Care in a few days.

An hour or so later, the unit clerk called out to her. "Serena?''

She glanced up from her paperwork.

"There's another cop down in the waiting room, asking to see Grant."

Serena lifted an irritated eyebrow and glanced at the time. "At this hour? Well, I suppose they work odd shifts, so go ahead and let him in."

Intent on her work, she didn't see the officer go into Grant's room. She finished her note, then crossed the hall to give the officer an update on Grant's condition.

The figure bending over Grant's bedside brought her up short. The cop was female, with long, wavy brunette hair. Serena swallowed a gasp. The woman in the picture she'd glimpsed in Grant's wallet.

Serena almost spun around on her heel to leave them alone. She wanted to be anywhere but watching this. But she forced herself to stay put. Clearly, this woman meant something to him. Whoever the brunette was, she'd want an update on Grant's condition.

Serena took a step into the room, pasting a bright smile on her face. "Can I help you?"

The woman whirled at the sound of her voice, thrusting her hands into her pockets and flashing Serena a sorrowful look. "Are you Grant's nurse? Can you tell me how he's doing?"

"Yes, my name is Serena. His condition has stabilized."

"Loren." The brunette introduced herself in return. "I don't understand. Why isn't he awake yet?"

Serena shrugged. Her gaze dropped down to Loren's left hand. She didn't know why the absence of a ring made her feel better. For all she knew, Grant already had another ring bought and paid for, just waiting for the right time to pop the question. She tore her mind from her traitorous thoughts. "I know this is difficult. He'll wake up when his body is ready."

"Does he know I'm here?" Serena could see the skepticism in the other woman's gaze.

"It's possible. Hearing is the last sense to go and the first to return. Often patients tell me how they heard me talking to them long before they were able to respond." Serena wondered if Grant would react to the sound of Loren's voice better than he had to hers. She shoved aside another wave of jealousy. "Go ahead and talk to him."

"I'm here, Grant." Loren spoke so softly, Serena wasn't sure he'd be able to hear over the noisy unit activity. "Please, get better soon. I miss you."

The words cut deep. Serena had suspected the worst when she'd stumbled across the picture, but seeing the reality of the closeness of their relationship was worse.

Much, much worse.

"Are you all right?" Loren was actually looking at her with concern.

Serena forced herself to give a jerky nod. "I…have to go. You can stay only a few minutes. Grant needs his sleep."

"I understand." Loren backed away from Grant's bedside. She looked pale, as if she might be feeling ill. "If—when he wakes up, will you tell him I was here?"

"Sure." She followed the other woman from the room, her mind still reeling from the shock of seeing them together. She'd always known that Grant had wanted to settle down. To eventually have a family. Hadn't they both spent hours planning their own? This wasn't Grant's fault. She had been the one who'd broken their engagement, not the other way around. Obviously, Loren, a cop herself, didn't mind his chosen profession.

The truth didn't offer one bit of comfort.

Luckily, her dual patient load kept her too busy to brood. Hard work and long hours had been her salvation once before. She was sure the strategy would work again. During the next lull in activity, Serena tried once more to see if she could rouse Grant. Trying not to think about Loren taking her place in Grant's life, she slipped her hand into his. She almost fell over when his fingers curled around hers in a firm grip.

The movement was probably pure reflex, yet Serena couldn't help feeling encouraged by his strength. She left one hand in his while the other stroked the upper part of his arm lightly. The hard muscle beneath her fingertips was achingly familiar.

"Grant, can you hear me? You had emergency surgery last night, but you're doing much better now. We're just waiting for you to wake up then we can take that nasty breathing tube out of your throat."

Serena paused, staring down at their joined hands, but whatever movement she'd noted earlier was absent now. His bluntly callused fingers were relaxed, far too pale against the sheets.

"I'm sure that tube hurts like heck, but you won't be able to talk until it comes out." Serena could barely speak past the lump of emotion that welled in her throat.

She waited a heartbeat, swallowing hard before asking softly, "Grant, can you open your eyes for me? Please?"

The voice of his angel was back and this time he was determined not to lose it. The pain still rolled over him in waves, but he determinedly fought it back. He grasped the hand near his as if it were a lifeline and concentrated on the voice.

He became aware of the breathing tube she'd talked about and fought down a surge of panic at her words. Easy now, one step at a time—he wanted to see the woman whose voice brought him out of the darkness.

Grant pried his eyelids open and a blurred face swam in the dim light above his head. He blinked once, and then again as slowly the features cleared. A beautiful face, classic cheekbones framed with riotous red-gold curls, familiar luminous blue eyes...

Serena.

CHAPTER FOUR

SERENA almost laughed out loud when Grant's eyes opened for the first time, and while he blinked in an attempt to focus she gently encouraged him.

"That's right. Look at me, Grant. You're in the hospital." Her voice cracked and she swiped away a stray tear, trying to remember all the things she needed to tell him now that she knew he was awake. "You had surgery last night. The doctor removed a portion of your lung and repaired the muscle in your left thigh. Everything went fine, just don't try to move around too much yet."

Grant held onto Serena's hand tightly as he continued to stare at her. She knew he couldn't speak and simply holding his hand in hers was enough. Then she suddenly remembered his sister, sitting in the quiet room all alone. "I forgot to mention that Cheryl is here, too. She'll be glad to see you're awake. I'll call her for you right now."

Serena moved as if to pull away, but Grant grew extremely agitated, tightening his grip. Serena looked down into his achingly familiar smoky gray eyes, wishing she could ease his distress.

"Grant, I promise I won't leave you alone. I just

want to call Cheryl. She's very worried about you. Give me two minutes and I swear I'll be right back.''

This time Grant relaxed against the pillow and Serena squeezed his hand reassuringly before letting go. She hurried to make the call. Cheryl promised to be in shortly and Serena returned to Grant's bedside to find that he was still awake, gazing at the variety of equipment that hung around his bed.

But when his gaze met hers she read the reproach in his eyes, as if he were upset with the fact she was taking care of him. Her enthusiasm faded fast.

What had she done?

Serena was his nurse. How had that happened? She'd avoided trauma patients since Eric's death. Dammit, she shouldn't be here. He'd let her walk away, hadn't he? Just to spare her seeing him busted up like this. To find that hers was the voice that had pulled him from the black hole of pain was a cruel, cruel joke. Why had fate chosen to throw them together now, after all this time?

The tension in Grant's room suffocated Serena to the point where she couldn't take a normal breath. Why on earth had she offered to work these extra shifts? Had she lost her mind? She'd thought she was doing a good thing by taking care of Grant, but obviously his feelings toward her hadn't changed in the past eighteen months. Somehow she hadn't anticipated Grant's negative reaction to seeing her again.

Straightening her shoulders, Serena inwardly swallowed her ire. Heck, it wasn't her fault that she'd been pulled down to the trauma room the night he'd happened to get himself shot. Given her druthers, she'd have chosen to swim naked in a pool of piranhas over the task she'd been assigned.

Besides, if this situation was anyone's fault, it was Grant's. He shouldn't have gone to a dangerous crime scene without wearing his flak jacket. The leg wound had been bad, but not compared to his chest wound. Trinity was the only level-one trauma center in the city. All trauma victims were brought there.

Cheryl must have noticed the stiffness between them, but didn't comment. Using his sister as a buffer, Serena encouraged Cheryl to spend as much time as possible with Grant. Her shift dragged by slowly. She almost asked Dana to switch patients, but that would have given rise to more questions than she cared to answer. Clearly Grant still resented her for walking away from their engagement. So what? She resented him for not loving her enough to change his career. Especially after Eric's death.

As her shift wore on Grant grew more agitated. Serena suspected he was too awake for that breathing tube and knew he wanted it out. Unfortunately, he needed to wait until the doctor made rounds.

Finally, she had no choice but to give him more morphine to calm him down. If he continued to struggle like that, he'd rip open the sutures or disconnect his IV. Giving him additional pain medication was walking a fine line, especially if he wanted that breathing tube out. He needed to be awake and co-operative when the doctors arrived.

When Dr. Hardy came in shortly thereafter, Serena was relieved to find that Grant was more comfortable but not completely zonked.

"I see our patient is awake." Dr. Hardy had a bad habit of talking over the patient, addressing the nurse as if the patient was too stupid to understand. Serena saw Grant's gaze narrow with irritation and quickly tried to intervene.

"Yes, and I happen to have his weaning parameters right here." She handed him the clipboard. "They look pretty good. I'm sure Detective Sullivan would like to get that breathing tube out."

"Hmm…" Dr. Hardy looked over the clipboard and then granted his permission. "OK, go ahead. Just make sure he keeps up the breathing treatments. I don't want him to crash with pneumonia."

Serena tried not to wince at the cardiothoracic surgeon's blunt words, especially since Grant was looking right at her, gauging her facial expressions.

She called in the respiratory therapist to assist. She gave Grant a few brief instructions, then, on the count of three, they pulled the tube out and instantly covered Grant's mouth and nose with an oxygen mask.

"Water…" Grant tried to speak, but his throat felt as if it were on fire. Luckily Serena knew exactly what he wanted and she reached for a plastic cup on his bedside table.

''Ice chips,'' she corrected. ''No water until Dr. Hardy gives permission.''

Grant frowned but took the few ice chips she offered him. He hated the fact that he had to be fed, resented even more that Serena was the one feeding him.

Pain washed over him with every breath he took, engulfing his brain in a dense fog. He supposed part of the haze could be due to the effect of whatever medicine Serena had given him. Either way, he didn't like struggling with the effort of putting a sentence together. He was relieved the tube was out but there were still dozens of wires and tubes holding him hostage.

With a scowl he leaned back against the pillows. Serena hovered near his bedside and he was tempted to ask her to leave. He knew she was as uncomfortable with the situation as he was. Lifting the cup of ice chips by himself took an almost monumental effort. On his first try he dribbled a few down his front and inwardly swore when the ice instantly melted on his skin. The second attempt went better and he managed to get a few more into his mouth. Except that they slid down his raw throat too quickly.

He coughed. A red-hot branding iron of pain seared his chest. Instinctively he grabbed at his incision, but Serena's hands were already there, applying pressure.

''Easy now.'' By holding pressure against the incision, it amazingly helped ease his pain. ''Coughing is good for your lungs, but choking on ice chips is definitely not.''

Her hands were awfully small under his, yet he'd felt their strength as they'd cared for him. He still couldn't believe that Serena was the angel who had pulled him out of the darkness. When he'd first seen her bending over him, he'd wondered if his imagination was playing tricks on him. She'd often haunted his dreams. But when she'd continued to smile down at him, he'd known she was real.

He'd always known that Serena was more than capable in her chosen profession, but he resented the fact that she was taking care of him while he lay helpless. Any minute he expected her to start in again on the dangers of his career, rubbing in how she'd been right all along.

The wound in his thigh throbbed painfully. Grant glanced down at the skimpy hospital gown barely covering the lower half of his body. Hell. They didn't even let you wear boxer shorts in this place.

''Why you?'' he asked when he could breath again with less discomfort. For a long moment she hesitated, then shrugged, dropping her gaze.

''I was on call the night they brought you in. Do you remember being shot?''

Grant closed his eyes. He vaguely remembered lights flashing. A body lying in the road. Moving shadows. A gun. Piercing pain.

Damn. He'd have given anything to spare Serena the harsh truth. He knew only too well how this was her worst nightmare. Given the same set of circumstances, though, he figured he'd make the same decision again. Any cop on the force would have done the same for him.

"I didn't recognize you at first, there was so much blood," she continued, when he couldn't speak. "When I realized who you were, I had no choice but to treat you like any other patient. We almost lost you, but somehow Dr. Hardy worked miracles in the operating room." She flashed him a lopsided grin. "That's why we put up with his obnoxious bedside manner."

He couldn't hold onto his resentment, one corner of his mouth kicking up in a weary grin. What did it matter that Serena was here? He had more important things to worry about. The gang activity had reached a new level of danger. He wanted to talk to the captain, as much as he could with his sore throat.

"Ted Reichert." His voice was so hoarse he barely recognized it.

Serena looked puzzled for a moment, then her brow cleared. "Oh, you mean the captain? I think he's planning to stop by later this morning, or did you want me to call him for you?"

"Call—please."

"It's only six-thirty," she warned.

He nodded. Serena did as he'd asked, returning after a few minutes. "OK, he's on his way in. Although I have to tell you he doesn't exactly sound like a morning person."

Grant merely shook his head, saving what was left of his voice. No, the captain wasn't a morning person. Hell, he wasn't an afternoon or a night person. Despite his gruff manner, though, Reichert cared about the officers under his command.

"Do you want me to call Cheryl back in?" Serena broke the silence that stretched between them.

He nodded his agreement. Serena had asked his sister to leave while they took out the tube.

Cheryl greeted him with a watery smile, leaning over the rail to give him a brief hug. "Thank God, Grant. Thank God you're all right."

Grant awkwardly patted her on the back, his arm hampered by the IV tubing in his forearm. "Cherrie. Where's David? The kids?"

"Back in Denver." Cheryl sniffled loudly. "I didn't think they would allow kids in here and I didn't have time to make elaborate arrangements. They didn't sound too confident that you were going to make it."

"I'm fine." He dismissed his various wounds. "Go home to your family."

"I'll go when I'm sure you're safely on your way out of here." She glanced over to where Serena sat outside the door, scribbling in his chart. "Serena, do you have any idea how much longer he'll stay in Intensive Care?"

Just then they were interrupted by a loud commotion next door.

"Who's that?" Grant frowned as two cops began

to argue over whether the patient in the bed needed
to be chained to the bed with ankle bracelets. Each
officer had a different opinion, their raised voices carrying through to his room.

"That's Jason, the kid who shot you." Cheryl's
eyes were grim.

Grant raised his eyebrows and turned his head to
look through the glass wall of his room. A mixed-
race adolescent boy sat up in the bed, which had been
loaded up with supplies as if he was going on a trip.
He expressed his opinion in a loud voice, not that
anyone paid a bit of attention to him.

Fortunately the captain arrived on the scene to
bring an end to the debate. "Cuff him."

Grant continued to stare, searching his memory.
The kid didn't look familiar, but obviously he must
have exchanged shots with him. He couldn't remember anything that might give him a clue as to which
gang he belonged to, if any. Grant barely remembered
the events surrounding the shooting, and he desperately wanted to find out what had happened.

"Hey, Sullivan, you look like hell." The captain
greeted him with his usual cheerful disposition.

"Thanks." Grant took a few more ice chips to wet
his parched throat. Already his strength was fading
fast. "Fill me in."

Ted Reichert dropped his heavy bulk into a chair
next to Grant's bed, one hand unconsciously rubbing
the center of his chest. "You tell me. Our guys arrived on the scene to find you bleeding and a rookie

named Joe Vine dead. Then, of course, we found that punk Jason, wounded from your gunfire.''

''Joe's partner?'' He pushed the question past his throat.

The captain rubbed his jaw. ''He showed up ten minutes later, out of breath. Said he chased another guy with a gun but lost him.''

Grant wrinkled his brow in an effort to concentrate. ''So what is all this? Increased gang activity? Dammit, when did they stop shooting each other?''

Ted Reichert shrugged. ''I don't know. But if this is their new trend, we need to put a plug in their plan, and quick. I have several officers working on this already. We'll get them. You don't have anything to worry about.''

His job always brought worry but clearly others were doing the legwork for him. Grant momentarily closed his eyes, fighting exhaustion. He wished he could help in some way. But, dammit, he didn't have the strength of a gnat.

''We'll take care of this.'' The captain spoke with resounding conviction. ''Your job is only to get yourself healthy enough to be sprung from this joint. We need you, Sullivan. You're one of the best detectives we have.''

Grant caught Serena's gaze, noting her face had grown somber as the captain spoke. He knew his boss was only reaffirming her worst fears. His job was important. Her fears were understandable, but also irrational. He forced himself to keep his tone light. "Yeah. Getting out of here is top priority."

Ted nodded brusquely, then turned to Serena. "I appreciate your support the other night, but I must admit you have your work cut out for you. He won't be a co-operative patient."

"I'm already aware of that," Serena responded tartly. She glanced pointedly at her watch and turned to Grant. "I have to give a report to the next shift. Is there anything else I can get you before I go?"

"A large glass of water."

Serena picked up the small plastic cup. "A small cup of ice chips coming right up."

Grant scowled at her retreating back, enjoying the sight of her slightly swaying backside a little too much. Despite the pain, he experienced the familiar stirrings of attraction. Serena's baggy blue scrubs hid her figure and he wondered if she'd changed over the last year and a half. She'd worked hard during the night, but still managed to look as fresh as if she had just started her shift. He could sit here for hours, listening to the melody of her voice.

He remembered how he'd loved to loosen the elastic band from Serena's red-gold curls, allowing them to tumble over her shoulders. Her hair would feel like spun silk against his skin. He'd lean down and bury his face in the fragrant mass, kissing her nape.

He shifted and a shaft of pain shattered his fantasy. He had no business thinking of Serena in an intimate way. She didn't belong to him. She had her life and he had his.

With a guilty start he remembered Loren. Rubbing a hand over the stubble on his cheeks, he wondered if he should ask someone to give Loren a call. Loren DuWayne was a fellow cop, his partner's widow. He'd kept in touch with Loren and her son Ben after Rick had died a few years ago.

They'd always been friends, although since his break-up with Serena he'd seen her more frequently. Recently, Loren had subtly made it clear that she was ready for more. He enjoyed spending time with Loren and her son, but something had held him back from taking that next step in their relationship. At first she'd been a sounding board after Serena had called off their engagement. In many ways, Loren was perfect for him. She was as dedicated to her job as he was to his. In spite of losing her husband to the risks of their career, she wouldn't make unreasonable demands like Serena had.

But seeing Serena again, having his body respond to her slightest touch, reinforced the truth. He wasn't immune to her, even after all this time. He couldn't in good conscience get involved with anyone else. Especially not a woman with a son that might grow dependent on him.

Serena stopped by his room one last time before she left. "Just thought I'd say goodbye. I'm working tonight, but you might convince Dr. Hardy to let you out of here before then."

"I'll try. First he has to talk to me like a person."
Grant didn't bother to hide his distaste of the arrogant
surgeon. "You'll be here tonight?"

Serena nodded. "I'm off after this weekend." With
a polite smile she turned away.

"Serena?" Grant called out before she could leave.

She paused in the doorway, shooting an expectant
glance over her shoulder.

"Thanks. Thanks for everything."

Serena acknowledged his thanks with another
smile, but surprise was also clearly reflected on her
features. Obviously she hadn't expected any appre-
ciation from him. Grant felt another flash of guilt at
making his displeasure so clear. He watched her walk
away, wondering exactly why he wanted to beg her
to stay.

The rest of the day passed tediously. He wasn't strong
enough to do much and grew irritated at how he
dozed off when he least expected it. The day shift
nurse agreed to his request and called Loren, inform-
ing him that she'd be in later that afternoon. He
should have looked forward to her visit, but instead
he wished she wouldn't make the trip.

Grant tried to send Cheryl home again, but she
stubbornly refused. The infamous Dr. Hardy didn't
bother to show his face either, so Grant didn't have
anyone on whom to take out his bad temper.

A few of the guys from the precinct showed up,
which helped relieve his boredom for a while. They
joked around and filled him in on the latest gossip.
They relaxed their hospital vigilance in the waiting

room once it became apparent that he was going to survive. But as they left, they informed him that the funeral for the dead rookie was going to be held the next evening. Grant became annoyed all over again when he realized he couldn't attend.

Loren stopped in to see him as promised. She hesitantly approached his bed, in awe of all the equipment that surrounded him. She leaned over the bed rail to brush his forehead with a friendly kiss. "Grant. I can't believe you're really all right."

Grant gave her his best reassuring grin, which came out more like a grimace. "I'm fine. They'll let me go in a few days."

Loren shot him a skeptical look. "Yeah, sure. I had to hog-tie Ben to his grandmother in the waiting room to keep him from following me."

Grant smiled. Ben was a great kid. "Oh, yeah?"

"He wants to see that you're alive with his own eyes." Loren dropped her gaze from his, toying with the zipper of her jacket. "I think he's afraid you're just going to disappear one day, like his dad did."

Grant's heart clenched at the thought of the little boy worrying about him. Both Loren and Ben had suffered enough, struggling to make it on their own. Poor kid. Grant knew things hadn't been easy for them. "Sneak him in here. I don't care what the hospital rules are. See if one of the guys can help cover."

Loren looked doubtful for a moment, then gave in. "Are you sure you don't mind?"

"I'll mind if you don't," Grant countered. "I want to see him, too."

A few minutes later, Loren tiptoed through the unit,

using one of their fellow officers to shield Ben. In his room, she set the boy on his feet. Grant knew that Ben looked up to him like a father figure, especially since his father had died while he'd just been a baby. The kid practically hung on his every word.

The little boy didn't seem to notice all the high-tech machinery. He took one look at Grant and ran to his side. Grant responded by reaching his left arm over the side of the bed to awkwardly embrace the boy he'd grown to love like a son.

"Mom said you were shot." His big green eyes were wide with awe.

"I guess." Grant grimaced at the morbid glee on the boy's features. "So what have you been up to? Getting ready for Little League?"

Ben nodded, trying to crawl up the side of the metal bed frame to sit on his lap. Loren pushed away from the door to intercept his acrobatic feat.

"Hey, big guy." She swung him to the floor. "That's a sure way to get us kicked out of here."

"But I haven't seen Grant in a really, really long time, Mom," Ben protested dramatically.

Grant reached over to place his hand on the boy's head. "Right now I'm pretty banged up. But when they let me out of here, you and I can spend some quality R and R."

Ben frowned. "What's that?"

Loren let out a tired laugh. "R and R stands for rest and relaxation, two things you know nothing about." She flashed Grant an apologetic smile. "I don't think Ben's going to be happy until you can play ball with him again."

Ben filled him in on his latest T-ball game, until Grant's nurse realized her visiting rules were being violated. She came in with a dark frown furrowed between her brows.

"I'm sorry, but no children allowed," she told them firmly. "I'm afraid I need to ask you to leave."

Loren apologized sweetly. As Ben gave Grant one last hug, she shot him a wink over her shoulder and mouthed the word, "Thanks."

Grant nodded understandingly. "I'll call you later," he promised, watching as they left. Sinking back against the pillows, he thought about his relationship with Loren. For the first time he wondered if he would have continued to date her, if not for the budding relationship he'd built with her son.

Once he'd planned on having a family with Serena. He understood that being a father was a time-consuming business, but he'd figured they'd find a way to make it work. Since their break-up he'd found himself drawn to Loren and Ben. He honestly looked forward to Ben's baseball games. But now the nagging doubt wouldn't leave him alone.

Had he tried to replace Serena's love with that of a ready-made family?

CHAPTER FIVE

"RICO, we need to talk." After coming upstairs, Serena caught the boy sneaking into his apartment, but this time she was quicker. She snagged him by his threadbare army green jacket before he could disappear.

The boy glared at her over his shoulder. She didn't ease up on her grip but steered him purposefully into her apartment.

"About what?" Shaking loose of her hold, he dropped negligently into one of her kitchen chairs, crossing his arms defiantly across his chest.

She sighed. She really wasn't in the mood for this.

"Want something to eat?" Serena wearily pulled a bowl of cereal and some milk from her fridge.

The flash of hunger in his eyes gave him away. Wordlessly, she brought two bowls from the cupboard and slid one across the table to him.

For a moment they shared a companionable silence as they ate. Then Serena pushed her empty bowl aside and pinned him with an expectant look.

"What's going on?"

"Nuthin'." Mouth partially full of food, he gulped the last of his cereal. Noisily, he slurped the leftover milk.

"Don't give me that crap, Rico. Do you think I'm stupid? You're hanging out with bad kids. Why?"

"They're not bad. They're my friends." He thrust his jaw out stubbornly.

"Friends don't play with weapons, Rico. Which gang are you hanging with? The Hombres? Or the Spikes?"

Startled, he stared at her. He obviously hadn't expected her to have any knowledge of the gangs, much less know their names. Serena wanted to shake him until his brains rattled in that pitiful excuse for a head.

"I'm not hanging with any gang," he denied.

"I'm betting the Hombres. They wear green." She eyed his jacket pointedly then leaned forward. "I'll call the police, Rico. You'll go to jail. Marta will cry. Is that what you want?"

His expression went carefully blank. "Go ahead. I don't care."

Helpless, Serena sighed. How could she convince him to see the truth? "Do you want to know why I know the names of the gangs? Because I see their wounded. Knife injuries because they like to aim for the gut. Maimings, especially missing fingers and toes, one of their specialties. And my personal favorite, gunshot wounds. They like to shoot people in the back of the head, execution style. The kid that was brought in a few weeks ago died. Is that what you're looking for, Rico? The thrill of courting death?"

He dropped his gaze, but remained silent. Was he

shutting her out? Or had her words sunk in, even a little?

"The other night they brought in a kid who'd shot a cop. He's going to prison for a long time. The police will try him as an adult, even though he's only fifteen. His life is over." She reached over and grabbed his arm. "Listen to me. Stay away from the Hombres. Nothing good will come of them. Only pain and sadness. Marta loves you. Don't hurt her like this."

He idly kicked his legs against the chair, keeping his gaze on the floor. Finally, after what seemed like an hour, he glanced up at her.

"I'd never hurt my sister."

Serena swallowed hard. "I know you love her, Rico. She loves you, too. She worries when you stay out so late."

"I can take care of myself."

"That's right, you can. But you need to help take care of Marta, too. You're all she has left in the world."

He seemed surprised, as if he expected an argument. She knew better than to question his ability to take care of himself. After a few minutes, he thoughtfully nodded.

Serena was careful not to let her satisfaction show. Instead, she gestured to his empty cereal bowl. "Are you still hungry? I could make you some eggs."

He shook his head. "Nah. The cereal was fine."

"How about another time, then?" Serena quickly

made a mental inventory of her freezer. "Dinner. Tell Marta I'll cook spaghetti."

"OK." Rico slid from his chair. "I'll let her know."

"Great. See you later."

The boy dashed from her apartment. The door slammed shut behind him. Seconds later, she heard the sound of his apartment door opening then closing across the hall.

Mission accomplished, Serena thought with a sigh. Oh, she wasn't naïve enough to think she'd turned him completely around with one conversation, but she hoped Rico would stick closer to home at least for a while. Conjuring the image of a gunshot wound or knife wound in his wiry twelve-year-old body was too easy. She pushed up from the table, carrying their dirty dishes to the sink. Maybe she could talk to Grant about Rico. A cop might have more of an impact on his impressionable mind than a sympathetic neighbor.

Besides, Grant was good with kids. Especially boys.

The thought caused a familiar pain to cramp in her stomach and she bent at the waist, trying to catch her breath. The pain eased, but didn't let up completely.

Still clasping her stomach, Serena headed down the hall, pausing outside the door to the second bedroom. She placed her hand on the doorknob, but didn't go in.

For a moment she closed her eyes and leaned on the door frame. She'd been doing so well. The doctor had encouraged her to stay out of the room. Weeks had gone by without needing to go inside. Why now? Because of Grant? Because of the idea of him being a good father?

Deliberately she unclenched her fingers from the handle. Somehow she found the willpower to turn away. She knew by now there was no point in going back. Her efforts needed to be centered on moving forward. On living her life, not wallowing in the past.

She retreated to her bedroom, bone tired, her stomach hurting. There was nothing she could take for the pain because it wasn't physical but emotional. Sleep didn't come easily.

The sick certainty that she should have told Grant the truth months ago kept her awake for a long time.

Exhausted by the steady stream of visitors yet bored at the same time, Grant found himself glancing frequently at the clock between naps, waiting for the start of Serena's shift.

As upset as he'd been at first, he now looked forward to seeing her again. Grant told himself it was because she'd helped save his life, his guardian angel of sorts. Her dedication to her career had been one of the things he most liked about her. Their engagement had ended abruptly but maybe they could salvage something. Friendship, for starters.

Long hours later, Grant caught sight of Serena standing at the central nurses' station. Man, she was so beautiful. The phrase was trite but in her case so

very true. She'd pulled her red-gold hair into a ponytail, although little wisps escaped to curl around her
face. The baggy blue scrubs only emphasized her
slender figure. Had she lost weight over the past eighteen months? He frowned. He didn't like the thought
of Serena being stressed to the point of losing weight
she couldn't afford to lose.

She glanced up and caught him staring. Their gazes
locked. Then she smiled and nodded at him before
turning back to the chart she was reviewing with another nurse.

A strange sense of peace settled over him. He laid
his head back against the pillow with a sigh. She'd
told him she would return, but Grant had been half-
afraid she wouldn't show.

Now he could rest.

The beeping alarm of his IV woke him. He turned
toward the sound and saw Serena pushing buttons on
his IV pump.

Wait a minute. Not Serena, some other nurse. A
tall blonde. He frowned.

"Who are you?" His dry throat croaked with the
effort to speak.

"Hello." The nurse looked up from the IV pump
and smiled at him. "My name is Amy. I'm your nurse
for the shift."

He couldn't quell his panic. "But where's Serena?
I saw her a little while ago."

"She has a different patient assignment tonight,"

Amy explained patiently. "You've been sleeping for quite a while. I'm glad. Resting is good for you."

Now that he realized that Serena had chosen to take care of someone else, he didn't think he'd get any more rest. Was she avoiding him? He tried to curb his disappointment. "Please, ask Serena to come in and talk to me. Just for a few minutes."

"First I'll need to change your dressings, then I'll find Serena. She might be busy with her patients, though."

Grant gritted his teeth when Amy pulled the dressing off his chest incision. Damn, that hadn't hurt a bit when Serena had performed the task.

"This really looks great." Amy's tone held satisfaction. "No signs of infection."

Silently Grant nodded, although he really didn't care. He wanted her to hurry up already, so he could talk to Serena.

Amy left a few minutes later. Grant stared at the doorway, listening to the beeping on his heart monitor. The regular tone should have reassured him. Instead, his mind raced.

Why had Serena switched patient assignments? Because of his bad attitude when he'd first woken up? Or because she didn't want anything more to do with him? Maybe she really couldn't bear the sight of him, not when he'd come so close to leaving this earth for good.

"You wanted to talk to me?" Serena hovered in the doorway.

"Yes. Come in, please." He motioned her closer.

She came up to stand by the side of his bed, glancing over him anxiously. "Is there something wrong?"

"Yes. I was expecting you to take care of me."

Her eyebrows rose questioningly, then her gaze dropped to her hands. "I thought it would be best to take care of someone else tonight. Amy is an excellent nurse."

"Maybe, but she isn't you." Grant held out his hand, palm up. After a moment's hesitation, she placed her hand in his. Her small hand was strong and he squeezed it gently. "Your voice brought me back, Serena. I owe you my life. I didn't mean to react so strongly when I realized you were taking care of me."

A sad smile played along the corners of her mouth. "That's OK. I'm sure seeing me was quite a shock."

"Worse for you, though," Grant countered.

"Yes, it was." Serena squeezed his hand then pulled hers from his grip. She stepped away from the bed, putting more distance between them. "I'm sorry, Grant, but I can't stay long. My patient is only four hours post-op from open heart surgery. I need to keep a close eye on him."

"I understand." Grant really did understand, although he wanted to persuade her to stay. But one thing about Serena, she took her patient care seriously. Trying to consider the poor guy who'd had major surgery, he waved her off. "OK, then. If you wouldn't mind stopping in before you leave, I'd appreciate it.''

"I will." Serena flashed him another of her sad smiles. Had he put that sadness in her eyes? The thought was sobering. Toward the end of their engagement, he'd known she'd often been sad. But he'd been hurt as well. Why did he long to comfort her now?

Grant only caught glimpses of Serena throughout the rest of her shift. She was busy, he could see the way she hustled from one task to the other.

By early morning, though, he lost track of her. Dr. Hardy came in to give him the news he was being transferred to a ward. While he was grateful to be taking a step in the right direction, one thought overshadowed the others.

Serena hadn't come to say goodbye.

"I don't like the looks of that blood pressure," the resident commented from the doorway.

Serena didn't answer. She didn't exactly like Mr. Grayson's blood pressure either, but she was doing the best she could. She titrated his dobutamine up another notch and hung another bottle of albumin.

Mr. Grayson had taken a turn for the worst just as she was trying to give a report to the oncoming day shift nurse. Between the two of them, they labored over the patient, attempting to get him stabilized.

"Dr. Hardy is on his way," Judith told her. "He wants to see his I and O.''

"Too much output from his chest tube in the past hour," Serena noted as she examined the chest tube collection chamber. "He may need to go back to the OR."

As she spoke, Mr. Grayson's blood pressure dipped even further. Just then Dr. Hardy walked into the room.

"What's going on?" His features pulled into a dark scowl.

Serena was used to Dr. Hardy's black moods. She quickly rattled off what had transpired in the past hour.

"He's bleeding." Dr. Hardy glared at the blood filling the chest tube chamber as if the situation were the patient's fault. "He'll need to go back to the OR."

"Should we give him another two units of blood first?" Judith asked as she carried the two bags into the room.

"That would help." Sarcasm laced his words.

Serena ignored him, just like she ignored everything else that didn't directly impact her patient. But as she worked over Mr. Grayson, she wondered what Grant was thinking. Her shift had ended a good half-hour ago but she hadn't moved from this bedside for the past few hours.

"Hell. Forget about going to the OR. Get me the chest tray. We'll crack him open right here." Dr. Hardy was already shoving his arms into the sleeves of a sterile gown.

Serena had already brought the chest tray to the room earlier, the minute her patient's blood pressure had begun to dive downward. She donned her own gown and mask, then quickly opened the sterile tray.

Her heart pounded as Dr. Hardy quickly cut through the sternal incision. This type of bedside OR didn't happen every day in the ICU, but often enough that she'd been through this before. Judith brought additional supplies into the room as Dr. Hardy demanded, leaving Serena to act as his OR nurse.

Blood pooled everywhere, but Dr. Hardy finally found and repaired the bleeder. After another hour, he sutured his patient's chest closed. Mr. Grayson seemed to be holding his own.

"Let me know if there is the slightest change." Dr. Hardy tossed his soiled gown into the trash.

"I will." Serena helped clean up the mess as Judith quickly recorded the most recent set of vitals.

"So, do you really need a report?" Serena joked as she and Judith passed each other in the room.

"Nah, I think I can figure things out from here." Judith hauled the trash out of the way. "Thanks for sticking around, though. I appreciate the help."

"No problem." Serena scrubbed her hands and arms down at the sink. The metallic scent of blood couldn't be so easily erased. "Anything else before I go?"

"Nope, that's all for now."

"Good." Serena headed to the central nurses' station. She glanced into Grant's room, but it was empty.

One of their housekeepers was mopping the floor. When she looked back at the assignment board, she realized Grant's name had been wiped clean.

"Where did Grant Sullivan go?" Serena asked the unit secretary.

"They transferred him out. He's on the third floor surgical unit."

"Thanks." Dazed, Serena left. Grant had already been moved to a private room. Clearly she'd been too deeply immersed in Mr. Grayson's bleeding chest to see him leave.

The third floor surgical unit wasn't far, so she headed down the hall towards room number twenty-one. But she didn't find Grant in his room that time either. Once again, she went to the unit clerk.

"I'm looking for Grant Sullivan, he's in room twenty-one."

"Oh, you just missed him. They took him down to Radiology for some tests. Should be back in an hour or so."

Serena nearly swayed on her feet. Another hour? No way would she last that long. She already needed to prop her eyelids open with her fingernails. "Thanks. I'll come back later."

Serena left the hospital to return home. Thankfully the ride was a short one. Exhausted, she climbed the stairs. Deep down, she acknowledged she wouldn't make the effort to see Grant later. Maybe this way was best.

A clean break was probably easier for both of them.

CHAPTER SIX

HER impromptu meal with Marta and Rico went well and afterwards Marta thanked Serena for taking the time to talk to Rico.

"I don't mind, Marta." Serena gave her friend a hug. "He's basically a good kid. Just a little lost in his search for friends."

"I wish I could be home more," Marta sighed. "But we wouldn't survive on minimum wage."

"Marta, there's a program at Trinity that helps you go back to school to become a nurse, if you work there. It's their response to the nursing shortage. Maybe you should think about it. Even if you only worked in the kitchen or as a runner, you'd be eligible for the program."

"Hmm. I'll check it out," Marta promised.

When Serena kept herself busy, she didn't think about Grant. But alone at night in her wide bed, the memories would come.

She and Grant had been so good together. From the first time she'd met him, she'd felt an instant connection. A magnetic pull that she could only explain as chemistry. Sure, the physical attraction was there, but this was something deeper. Something instinctive. Elemental.

Stop torturing yourself, she told herself firmly. You know he's not the right man for you. Serena turned over and punched a fist into her pillow. Grant Sullivan had no right interrupting her sleep.

After a few days of battling restlessness, though, she couldn't stand it any more. She needed to know Grant was safely on the road to recovery. Serena was scheduled to go into Trinity for a required in-service on new trends in managing trauma. Arriving early, she headed up to Grant's room.

The patient in the bed glanced up when she came in, but the patient was a woman.

"Oh, I'm so sorry." Face flushed, Serena quickly backed out of the room. "My mistake."

"No problem," the woman called out.

She headed over to the nurses' station. "Will you, please, tell me where Grant Sullivan is?"

"He went home earlier today." The unit secretary appeared to be drowning in paperwork and didn't look up from her computer. "That's all I know."

"Thanks." Serena headed downstairs for her class.

But while the information on the latest treatment protocols for blunt trauma was interesting, she couldn't concentrate. How had Grant managed to get discharged so quickly? Did he have someone at home to help him out?

Loren perhaps?

An hour and a half later, Serena was thankful to escape Trinity. Once in her car, she found herself driving toward Grant's house.

She didn't know if he still lived in the small bungalow he'd bought before they'd met. But as she slowly drove down the street, she noticed his old familiar rusted blue Chevy was parked in the driveway.

OK, he must still live there because no one else would drive a twenty-year-old car that was so rusted you could hear water sloshing in the trunk when it rained. She circled the block then slowly drove past his house again then admonished herself for being an idiot. She pulled up to the curb and parked.

Bravely she walked up the sidewalk to the front door. Once Grant had given her a key. But that had been a lifetime ago. Feeling foolish, she rang the doorbell.

Muffled sounds could be heard from deep inside the house. Several seconds passed. Was Grant physically unable to make it to the door? Should she walk in?

Or maybe he wasn't alone? Her stomach twisted in a tight knot. She'd just convinced herself to leave when the door swung open.

Grant stood, leaning heavily on the door frame. He looked more like his old self, wearing a pair of baggy sweats and a ragged navy blue Milwaukee Police Department T-shirt. His hair was mussed, his cheeks gaunt.

"Serena." Surprise widened his eyes. "Come on in."

"How are you, Grant?" She stepped over the threshold and glanced around the interior of his living

room. He had new furniture, the black leather sofa-
love seat combination that he'd always wanted. When
they'd been planning their life together, she'd agreed
to leather but had begged for any color other than
black. There was a blanket and pillow lying on the
sofa and Grant headed back there, gesturing for her
to sit down.

"I was at the hospital today for an in-service and
found out you were discharged." Serena perched on
the edge of her seat and clasped her hands in her lap.

"Yeah, it's great to be home." He leaned back
against the pillow and closed his eyes with a sigh.

His face was flushed and Serena frowned as she
leaned forward to examine him more closely. His lips
were pale and he appeared exhausted. Just from getting up to answer the door? Didn't seem right.

"Grant, how are you feeling?"

He pried one eye open to peer at her. "Fine. Other
than a whopping headache."

The nagging feeling at the back of her neck intensified. She rose from her seat to kneel beside him.
Laying a hand on his forehead, she gasped when his
skin felt hot to her touch. "You have a fever," she
accused. "How on earth did you manage to get discharged with a fever?"

He closed his eye and sighed. "I didn't have a
fever this morning."

"This just started in the past few hours?" Serena
sat back on her heels and glanced at her watch. The

time was nearly four in the afternoon. "We need to call your doctor."

"No. I'm sure I'll be fine in a few hours."

"Grant, this isn't funny. One of your incisions could be infected. Or maybe your lungs have begun to develop pneumonia." She fought the urge to stroke his chest. Her stethoscope was in her car. She debated running out to grab it.

"So check the incisions if you want." Grant shifted slightly on the sofa, then pulled up his shirt to expose his chest wound.

"I will." Had he thought she wouldn't take him up on his offer? She'd put up with the most arrogant of surgeons. One cranky cop was hardly a challenge. "Hang tight, I'm pulling off the tape."

She eased the dressing away from his skin. The area around the incision was a little red, but the wound appeared clean. No sign of purulent drainage, no foul odors.

"How come that doesn't hurt when you do it?" Grant asked sleepily.

She had no idea what he was babbling about. "This one looks fine." She replaced the dressing, and glanced at his long muscular legs hidden from view beneath the sweatpants. "What about your thigh injury?"

That question made his eyes pop open. "What about it?"

"Could that one be infected?" Serena didn't want to ask him to drop his pants but she refused to leave him in this state. Infections were nothing to mess around with. Too bad if the fact that Grant was wearing clothes rather than the impersonal hospital gown made the setting more intimate than it should have been.

"Forget it." Grant avoided her gaze. "The home health nurse is stopping in tomorrow. She can look at it then."

"I'm not leaving until I've seen the wound for myself." If Grant thought he could beat her at a duel of stubbornness, he was wrong. "We can do this the easy way or the hard way, take your pick."

"Oh, yeah? What's the hard way?" Despite his flushed skin and his over-bright eyes, he flashed her a cheeky grin.

Serena felt her lips curve in an answering smile. "Wrestling is the hard way. And, believe me, in your condition it's no contest. I'll win."

"Sure, now you want to wrestle, when I'm as weak as a newborn kitten." Grant grimaced and shifted again. "Damn. My entire body aches too much to give that option a try. I'll give gracefully." His hands reached for his waistband.

Serena found herself holding her breath as he tugged the sweats down then eased the elastic over one hip, low enough to expose the white gauze covering his thigh dressing. She reminded herself that she was a professional and bent to the task at hand. But the firm muscle beneath her hands reminded her that she'd once had the privilege of touching him. Of holding him. Loving him.

The room turned hazy and she realized she was still holding her breath. Calming herself with several long deep breaths, she concentrated on the incision. This one didn't look nearly as neat and tidy, but after careful inspection she deemed there was no sign of infection.

"This looks good, too." She replaced the dressing then stood. "I'll be right back. My stethoscope is in my car."

"Serena, don't…"

She allowed the door to close behind her, cutting off his protest. Stubborn man. There was no way she was just going to leave him lying at home fresh out of the hospital suffering from a fever. How he'd managed to convince Dr. Hardy to let him go in the first place, she had no idea.

Moments later she let herself back in. Grant hadn't moved from his spot on the sofa. "I need you to take your shirt off."

"This just keeps getting better and better." Grant gamely pushed himself upright. "Only my shirt? Maybe you should do a thorough check on all body parts. You know, make sure they're functioning properly."

"Oh? Have you been suffering from a frustrating…problem? There's medication for that now, you know. I can recommend a specialist."

Grant bit back a laugh. This easy bantering had

been just one of the many things he'd missed with
Serena. She was bright, quick with a comeback when
he got out of line. Favoring his right side, he tried to
ease his shirt off. The tension on his incision hurt like
hell.

"Ouch." He grimaced and lowered his arm, covering the incision site. Pushing off the sofa, he stood.
"You'll need to help. I still can't raise this arm very
high."

"Here." She grabbed the hem of his shirt and
pulled it up over his head. A lightning bolt of pain
shot through his side and a low groan escaped his lips
as he swayed.

Serena quickly placed her hands on his hips to
steady him. He glanced down at her at the same moment she tipped her head to look up at him.

Close. They were so close that he could lean down
to kiss her with very little effort. Did she taste as
potent as he remembered? He ached to find out.

The moment stretched for ever. Good memories
rushed back, staggering him with their intensity. The
hours they'd spent talking and making love. The sheer
joy in her eyes when he'd proposed. The way she'd
jumped into his arms, laughing and crying at the same
time, planting kisses all over him. The plans they'd
made for the small church wedding she'd wanted.

Grant was hardly aware of reaching for her. But in
an instant she filled his arms and his mouth crushed
hers. Serena melted against him, as if they'd never

spent nearly two years apart, her soft lips parting in an invitation he couldn't resist.

He feasted on her, tongue delving deep. Her hands smoothed over his back and he nearly groaned with a sudden spurt of need. The need to possess her almost brought him to his knees. Stroking the soft skin around her neck, his fingers tangled in the wild curls of her hair. Nothing had ever felt so right.

The shrill ring of the phone caused Serena to jerk out of his grasp. He nearly tumbled backward onto the sofa. His answering-machine picked up on the second ring and the caller didn't leave a message, but the moment was lost. Staring at him, she pushed her tangled hair back from her face.

"Grant, I…" She swallowed hard. "You shouldn't have done that."

His breath sawed in and out of his lungs, and his knees threatened to buckle. But he couldn't stop himself from tracing a finger over the smattering of freckles across her nose.

"You kissed me back. I've missed you, Serena." God knew that was the truth. As much as he resented the way she'd refused to compromise, he'd never been able to forget her. At odd points during the day he'd think about her, chastising himself afterward. But against his will she'd followed him into his dreams, haunting him with her sweet smile and magical touch.

"I don't think Loren would appreciate hearing that."

He winced with guilt. He didn't know how Serena had found out about Loren but she was right. The friendship line between he and Loren hadn't been crossed, but Loren deserved to know the truth. Wrong or not, he wanted Serena with a desperation that refused to let him go. Why couldn't he feel this way with Loren? Cold reality killed his lingering desire quicker than any icy shower.

Setting her jaw sternly, Serena stepped away and reached for her stethoscope. All business now, she made him take several deep breaths while she listened, moving the drum of the stethoscope around his chest.

"I think you might need to cough and deep breathe more. And push fluids. I'll call your doctor." She rolled the stethoscope in her hands.

"Wait." Grant grasped her arm to prevent her from leaving. "We need to clear something up, Serena. Loren and I are just friends." And he'd call Loren again soon, to tell her exactly that. Stringing her along because he didn't want to hurt her son wasn't fair, to either of them. Not when a single kiss had forced him to realize how much he still ached for Serena. He tried not to sound too defensive. "She's had a tough time. She needed a helping hand. I was there for her, that's all."

"It's OK, Grant. Nothing's changed between us." Serena raised woeful blue eyes to his and his heart squeezed in his chest. "Sex was never the problem, was it? You're still a cop and I'll never love a hero."

"Serena..." Grant sank down on the edge of the sofa, fighting a swell of panic at the bleak expression in her gaze. "Let's talk, OK? Maybe there's a way—"

"I'm glad you found someone," she interrupted with a falsely bright smile. Her hands twisted the black tubing of her stethoscope until it looked like something alien. "Really. You deserve to be happy."

"So do you." Why was she being so stubborn about this? Didn't she know how rare and precious love was? Hell, she couldn't have kissed him like that if she didn't still feel something for him.

Could she?

"Yes, I do deserve to be happy." She surprised him by agreeing. "And that's the problem. I'll never be happy, married to a cop."

Grant absently rubbed the ache in his thigh and fought a shiver. So this was it, then. They'd gone full circle. Back to the beginning of the end. He couldn't deny that the blood of a true-blue, die-hard cop flowed through his veins.

Even now, when his head throbbed with fever, he itched to go through his reports. To search for clues, to examine the ballistics reports and dig into every minute detail surrounding this latest case. He wanted to comb the streets, isolating gang members to discover what was really going on. Who was the one behind the violence? Or were there several? Was this just some weird initiation rite or something far more sinister?

A rookie cop was dead. Everything he lived for, everything he believed in demanded that justice be served. Whoever was responsible needed to be punished.

He couldn't apologize for being who he was.

And there was no way Grant could give up his life, just to make Serena happy.

CHAPTER SEVEN

SERENA abruptly left Grant on the sofa, heading into the kitchen where she knew she'd find the phone. She set her tangled stethoscope aside. Pressing her palms flat on the counter, she tried to control the shaking. Her lips tingled from his kiss. Dear God, why now? Why had Grant kissed her like that? To remind her of what she'd missed? For eighteen months she'd managed to keep her basic needs in a deep freeze. Why had they once again thawed for the wrong man?

She understood that her feelings toward Grant's career weren't normal. Grant had called them irrational, which had hurt. He didn't seem to understand everything she'd gone through. Some women would have glamorized a cop's life, lured by the element of danger. No way was she one of them.

Her brother Eric had given his life to save a child. After the tragic death of their parents, Eric had been the only family she'd had left in the world. Blackened from smoke, he'd still been wearing his firefighter gear when he'd died in the trauma room at Trinity Medical. She could still envision his soot-streaked face. Eric had given everything he'd had to his job, at her expense.

Grant was the same way. Serena wanted someone

to come home to. Someone who would be there for her. Someone to help her raise a family.

The thought of having a family nearly brought tears to her eyes. So much had happened a year and a half ago. And while she'd buried the pain, it had never truly left her. Yet there was nothing to gain by wallowing in self-pity.

Besides, Grant hadn't sat around, waiting for her. He'd found someone who could share his risks when she couldn't. He claimed they were just friends, but she suspected Loren's feelings went far deeper than that. The idea of Loren at Grant's side shot a fresh shaft of regret straight to her heart.

Sadness gave way to anger. What was he thinking, to restart something they couldn't finish? Worse yet, why had she allowed herself to respond? She was smarter than that, wasn't she?

Certainly, she refused to be stupid enough to fall for Grant Sullivan's charm once again.

Serena notified Dr. Hardy's office. His nurse practitioner promised to have him return the call. Serena explained the situation but the nurse practitioner hadn't seemed deeply concerned about Grant's fever. Maybe she was overreacting. Slightly mollified, Serena returned to the living room.

Grant had fallen asleep on the sofa. For a moment she simply gazed at him. His sandy brown hair was longer than normal, brushing against his broad forehead. His features were relaxed, although she knew how intense his gaze could get, especially when deeply immersed in a case. His heroic nature was so much a part of him, she honestly understood he'd never change. It was unfair to ask him to.

Yet just like that first night in the hospital, she couldn't quite force herself to leave him. What was it about her that insisted on caring for those in need? Although Grant certainly didn't appear as ill as he had been, she wouldn't be satisfied until he was well on the road to recovery.

She settled down on the comfortable love seat across from him. Thirty minutes later, Dr. Hardy returned her call.

"How high is his fever?"

"Not too bad, just under 102." Serena glanced through the doorway at Grant. "The rest of his vitals are fine, although his heart rate is understandably higher than normal because of the fever. I examined his surgical sites, they both look really good. His lungs sound a bit coarse and distant in the left lower base."

"Is he taking the antibiotics I prescribed?"

Hmm. Good question. Serena swept her gaze around the kitchen, then craned her neck to peer into the living room. "I don't know for sure, but you can bet I'll find out."

"I also sent him home with a script for pain medication. Apparently, while Detective Sullivan was here, he continually refused to take them. Doesn't surprise me now to find out he isn't coughing and deep breathing as much as he should.'' Dr. Hardy definitely sounded annoyed.

''I'll talk to him. Anything else I should have him do, other than pushing fluids?'' Serena asked.

''No, but let me know if his fever isn't better by tomorrow.''

''Thanks for calling.'' Serena hung up the phone. Immediately, she searched for the prescriptions. Sure enough, she found the errant slips of paper, stuck between his discharge paperwork.

Of course, Grant hadn't bothered to get them filled.

Muttering under her breath, Serena took charge. Leaving Grant sleeping on the sofa, she drove to the nearest pharmacy to pick up his medications. Back at his house, she heated up some hearty chicken soup and carried everything into the living room on a tray.

''Grant, wake up.'' She shook his shoulder. ''Time for your medication.''

''Don't want any,'' he mumbled, half-asleep.

''You moron!'' Serena fought to control her temper. ''Not only did you neglect to take your antibiotics, but by refusing to take your pain medication you've made yourself worse.''

He blinked the sleep from his eyes. His gaze focused on the small amber medication bottles. ''Where did you get those?''

''Listen to me. Dr. Hardy returned my phone call. You can either co-operate with your care, which means taking your medication like you're supposed to, or you can go back to the hospital. Your choice. But eat first. You should take this antibiotic on a full stomach.''

Grant stared at the tray in her hands. ''Fine. You win. I'll take the antibiotic, but not the pain pills.''

''You'll take the pain pills or I'll force them down your throat,'' Serena threatened. ''Because once you've taken them, you're going to cough and deep-breathe, which is going to hurt like heck.''

Their gazes locked, both stubbornly refusing to give in.

''I can cough and deep-breathe without the pain pills.'' As if the matter were closed, he leaned forward to take the tray from her, setting it on his lap.

A red haze of fury blurred her vision. ''Dammit, Grant! Just take the pain medicine, will you? What in the heck are you trying to prove anyway? Superhuman strength?'' She rubbed a hand over her aching temple. ''God save me from stubborn heroes.''

Spoon halfway to his mouth, Grant stared at her as if shocked at her outburst. He shouldn't be shocked, she thought irritably. He'd always teased her about her red-headed temper. If anything, he should have known better than to push her buttons.

''You're breathtaking when you're angry.'' His voice was strained. ''I missed that, too, Serena.''

She didn't have an answer to that. Turning away, she walked back to the kitchen to pour a bowl of soup for herself. But instead of taking a tray of her own out to the living room to join him, she sat at the kitchen table.

Alone.

Grant hated to admit he felt much better after eating and taking the darned medication. He'd even given in enough to take one of the pain pills. Only half the recommended dose, but half was better than nothing in his mind.

Serena avoided him, and while he felt a little guilty for their argument, he knew that wasn't the real reason she kept her distance.

The physical awareness between them was a living, breathing thing, and refused to be ignored. True, Serena was giving it her best shot. He'd caught the yearning in her glance when she'd tended to his wounds. The old emotional baggage they'd carried had been dumped into a heap between them.

Grant struggled to his feet, intent on confronting her. Just then Serena breezed in.

"I'll take that." She grabbed the tray he'd been about to reach for. "Save your strength for the coughing and deep-breathing exercises."

"Gee, I can hardly wait." Grant kept his tone light, although he longed to pull her into his arms. Her musky scent lingered in the air long after she'd left. Damn, this was going to be tough. How could he convince her to give them a second chance? How long before she would put Eric's tragic death to rest? A few more weeks? Months? Another year?

When she returned several minutes later, she was all business again. They could have been in the hospital for all the distance she kept between them. At her instructions, he did several of the deep-breathing and coughing exercises. Then she instructed him to lie down on his non-injured side.

"Now what?" he asked warily, as he complied with her request.

"I'm going to beat on your chest." She knelt on the floor beside the sofa.

"Oh, is that all? Isn't just being here with you like this punishment enough?"

Serena stilled and dead silence filled the air. Grant inwardly swore. He'd meant to make a joke, but he should have bitten his tongue. Even if he had spoken the truth.

Being so close to Serena without having her was agonizing punishment. Every moment reinforced what they could have had together, if not for her irrational fears. But he was cruel to blame everything on her. The truth of the matter was, she'd been right.

His career *was* dangerous. A cop couldn't walk into a potentially deadly situation, thinking the worst would happen. He'd acted instinctively that night he'd been shot. He'd always followed his gut instinct.

He always would. No matter what the risk.

"I'm sorry. That wasn't exactly what I meant," Grant apologized softly.

"I know exactly what you meant." Serena's voice

was brittle. "This isn't easy for me either. Once I finish here, I'll leave."

Before he could say another word, she cupped her hands and lightly pounded on his chest. They'd done the same thing in the hospital when he'd been in the ICU, too, he remembered. The sensation wasn't painful, but it didn't feel great when she neared the area around his incision.

When she'd finished, she stood. He reached out to grasp her hand. "Don't go. Not like this."

"I have to." Serena's voice was strained. "We're not right for each other, Grant. We've been down this path before."

"Then why does this feel so right?" He tightened his grip when she tried to tug free. "Why does being with you feel exactly right? Are you trying to tell me you don't feel it too?"

"I do feel it." Her voice dropped to a mere whisper. "But we can't go back, Grant. Don't you see? Too much has changed. We can't go back."

With one last tug she broke free. She grabbed her stethoscope from the floor and hightailed it across the room. He could only watch helplessly as she left.

Too much had changed? What had she meant by that? Grant stared at his empty living room, the words echoing through his mind. There was something deeper going on with Serena. Something that drove a wedge between them.

He vowed to uncover the mystery. Because he

knew with a sick certainty that he and Serena didn't have a chance until he knew exactly what had changed for her.

That night, Serena tossed and turned in her sleep. Weeks had passed since she'd had the dream. Even as the image formed in her mind, she tried to stop the nightmare from returning. But her subconscious didn't listen. Flames shot from the upper windows of the house, dark hazy smoke obscuring the blue sky. She saw Eric stumble from the doorway, his face blackened by soot, holding a small child in his arms. He stumbled and fell to his knees, gasping for breath. Heart pounding, Serena ran toward him. But as she drew near he dropped the child onto the ground. Except it wasn't a child, but a small baby. Daniel? She reached for her son. Her dusky blue baby's face stared up at her. She snatched her hand back. Daniel wasn't breathing.

He was dead.

No! Daniel, please, don't die!

Serena bolted upright with a muffled cry. A fine sheen of sweat covered her body, her breath heaved from her lungs. She pried herself from the twisted damp linen and stumbled to the bathroom. Cupping her hands, she doused her face with cold water.

Nothing could change the irrevocable truth. Grant hadn't known about her pregnancy. When she'd begged him to quit the force, she'd only just discovered the news herself. And when he'd chosen his job over her love, she told herself it was for the best.

As the child had grown in her womb, so had her guilt over keeping her secret. But she'd been afraid that Grant would convince her to put up with his career for the sake of their child. When the premature labor pains had started in her seventh month, she'd immediately called the doctor. He'd admitted her into the hospital before she could blink. They'd hovered over her all night, giving her medication to stop the labor. But the pain had continued, and then the baby's heart rate had suddenly dropped and those little flutters of baby movement had stopped altogether.

The doctor had immediately performed an emergency C-section, but it had been too late. Her son had been stillborn. When she'd woken up, she'd sobbed and cradled the tiny baby to her chest, unwilling to understand why God continued to take those she loved. First her parents, then Eric and now her son. Serena had named the baby Daniel Eric and had insisted on a tiny grave for him.

The doctor tried to reassure her that this didn't mean that she couldn't try again to have a child. But Serena knew better. There'd be no other children with Grant.

The trauma of losing her child, after the twin shocks of Eric's death and her break-up with Grant, was more than she could handle. Serena teetered on the edge of a serious depression.

Dana tried to convince her to call Grant for help,

but she refused. Had she made the right decision? Would Grant have seen his job differently if he'd known about the baby? Serena honestly didn't know. Thankfully, she responded to treatment. Four months ago, she stopped the anti-depressants altogether. But just as she managed to get her life back on track, Grant rolled into the middle of it, on a hospital gurney, near death. And now she was reliving the past, all over again.

The nightmare had returned. And she knew the reason why. Grant had nearly died, without knowing about the son they'd created. The son who hadn't been strong enough to make it in this world.

One thought dominated all others. Despite the passage of time, Grant deserved to know the truth about his son.

CHAPTER EIGHT

A LOUD banging on her door woke her up late next morning. Several hours had passed last night before she'd finally dropped off to sleep. Groggy, Serena stumbled from her bed, swearing under her breath when her bare toes smacked the wood frame of her doorway.

"Serena!" Marta's frightened voice chased away the last remnants of sleep. She ignored her stinging toes. "Open up. Rico's hurt."

She flung open the door to find Marta anxiously bent over Rico's small frame lying half-propped against the wall between their apartments. His face was bloody, battered and bruised. Serena dropped to her knees. "Call 911, Marta. Now."

Marta sobbed but did Serena's bidding. Serena's heart squeezed as she examined Rico.

Gently, she lowered him to the floor so he was supine. He was unconscious and Serena was very worried about internal bleeding into his brain. His pulse was thready and his respirations were shallow. She pried one of his eyes open, then the other to examine his pupils' response to light.

They reacted, although she was concerned that the right side constricted slower than the left. She glanced down the apartment hallway towards the stairs. Where in the hell was the paramedic unit?

Marta stepped from Serena's apartment, leaving the door open. "Is he OK?"

"He's fine." Serena kept her voice firm. "Get me a cold washcloth. We'll take care of the worst of the blood."

With a jerky nod, Marta agreed and turned back inside. Serena couldn't have cared less about the blood, but at least the task gave Marta something to do. Quickly, she ran her hands along his limbs, searching for signs of other injuries.

The seven minutes they waited for the paramedics to arrive were the longest Serena could ever remember. When they thundered up the stairs, carrying a stretcher between them, Serena stepped aside gratefully.

"This is a twelve-year-old boy who was beaten primarily around the face and head. There are some bruises on his abdomen but nothing noted on his extremities. No limbs appear to be broken. He's remained unconscious and his last vitals were stable, except I couldn't check his blood pressure."

The two paramedics listened to her as they worked. They quickly hooked him to a heart monitor and rechecked the vital signs for themselves.

"Neuro status stable," one paramedic noted. He glanced at Serena and Marta. "Which one of you is his mother?"

"I'm his sister, his legal guardian." Marta bravely stepped forward. "Will he be all right?"

"Did you do this?" the paramedic asked coldly.

Marta paled as if he'd slapped her. Serena stepped forward and placed a stabilizing arm around Marta's slim shoulders. Marta trembled in her grasp, but her tone was fierce. "No! Of course not. I would never do this."

The paramedic's eyebrows raised questioningly. "Then who did?"

Serena had had enough. "We think he's been hanging with the Hombres. They are probably responsible for this. I've lived across from Marta and Rico for a year. Marta has never lifted a hand to Rico."

The rude man dropped his gaze, then worked with the other paramedic to strap Rico's unconscious form onto the stretcher, preparing to take him away.

"Wait," Marta cried. "Where are you going?"

"Trinity Medical Center." The quieter guy tossed the name over his shoulder. "You can meet us there." The two men wheeled the stretcher towards the stairs, then carried him down.

"We'll both go. I'll drive," Serena told Marta firmly.

The ER was busy when they arrived and Serena felt horrible for Marta as the poor girl was grilled over and over again about Rico's injuries before she was allowed in to see him. Serena continued to vouch for Marta, knowing how worried she'd be about the possibility of losing custody of her brother.

They waited while Rico was taken for a CT scan and subsequently to get radiology films taken. Finally they were allowed in to see him.

"Marta?" Rico was awake, but with his bruised face, he had difficulty speaking. His words were slurred.

"I'm here, Rico." Tears streamed down Marta's face. "You're going to be OK, do you hear me, *nino*? You're going to be fine."

"Rico, who did this to you?" Serena stepped closer to his bed, laying a hand on his skinny arm. "We have to notify the police."

"No." Rico shook his head, then whimpered. Marta stroked a hand over his brow. "Hurts."

Serena stifled a flash of sympathy. "Rico, the people here think Marta did this. If you don't tell the truth, then she may get in trouble." Serena knew full well that a young, barely twenty-one-year-old sister of a twelve-year-old was going to raise concerns. Her word on their behalf might not be enough to prevent Social Services from getting involved. And she couldn't imagine what some social worker would think of the long hours Marta worked between keeping two jobs.

Rico stared at Serena through puffy eyes already turning brilliant shades of black and blue. "Hombres. That's all I'm saying. No names. A group of Hombres did this to me."

*   *   *

The doctor admitted Rico to hospital to keep an eye on his concussion. So far the CT scan was negative for intracranial bleeding, but that could also change in the next twenty-four hours.

By the time Serena returned home, it was late. Too late to stop over at Grant's place to talk. And the next day, she was scheduled to work second shift in the trauma ICU at Trinity. Maybe she'd wait for a few days until Grant was feeling better. She couldn't shake him from her mind. Even while at the hospital with Rico and Marta, she'd wondered if Grant's fever had broken. Was he doing his coughing and deep-breathing exercises? Was he taking the pain pills? Or was he too stubborn to listen?

There was a home health nurse stopping in to take care of him, she reminded herself. *Stop thinking up excuses to go over there. He doesn't need you.*

But it took all her willpower not to succumb to her need to see him.

Grant waited for Serena to return, determined to get to the truth behind her shadowed eyes. But she didn't come near his door. Thankfully, his fever broke the next morning and each day he felt better and better.

Except for the damage to his thigh muscle, he was satisfied with his recovery. His thigh bothered him, though. He'd attended his physical therapy sessions religiously, but the young man who worked with him refused to comment on his chances of getting full strength back.

"That's a question for your doctor," was the frustrating reply.

Grant returned home after his afternoon session at the physical therapist and restlessly paced his living room. He could walk, but it was really more of a limp and hobble. One more day alone in this house and he'd go bonkers.

The doorbell chimed as if on cue. With a wry smile, he opened the door to find Ted Reichert standing there.

"Come on in, Captain." Grant opened the door wide. "I'm climbing the walls in here by myself."

"Glad to hear you're feeling better." Ted came into Grant's living room and settled on the sofa with a sigh. "I stopped by because I thought you'd want to hear the news from me first."

The somber expression in the captain's eyes put him on alert. "What is it?"

"Another cop was shot last night by a member of the Hombres gang."

Grant closed his eyes. "My God. Who? Will he be all right?"

"Jack Neuman and, yeah, he'll make it. We're waging a full-scale war against these kids, though. Stupid little punks."

"Do we know why the Hombres are shooting cops?"

"Yeah, we've busted a few and grilled them for a long time. Seems that this is some new gang initiation rite. Only they pair up, coming at the cop from two opposite sides to better their chances.''

Instantly, Grant remembered hearing from Dr. Hardy how his chest wound had been from the front, but his thigh wound had been from the back. For a moment he remembered shooting the guy with the gun, only to be hit from behind.

"I don't believe it." Grant shook his head. What in God's name would they think of next? "I want to help."

"Are you medically cleared yet?" the captain asked mildly.

Hell. "Not yet, but I can do office work. Wade through some of the autopsy reports. Match ballistics information."

"Look, Sullivan, we're on this. Don't worry about a thing. The sooner you get better, the sooner you'll be back on the team." The captain popped another antacid in his mouth, chewing noisily. "Just thought I'd let you know."

"Please, let me come down to the precinct, even for a few hours." Grant didn't like to beg, but this sitting around uselessly while gang members played target practice with cops was asking too much. Kids turning into killers. What in the hell was the world coming to?

"If I see you down at the precinct, I'll take your badge." The flash in the captain's eyes told Grant he wasn't kidding.

Helplessly, Grant watched as the captain trudged

down the driveway to the front curb where he'd parked his car. The older man slid behind the wheel and drove off, without so much as lifting a hand in a wave.

Grant gripped the door frame so tight the wood cut into the palm of his hand. Didn't the captain understand his heart and soul ached to help his comrades? Keeping the innocent of the city safe from scum like the Hombres was what he lived for. What was left if he didn't even have that?

The trauma ICU was hopping when Serena entered a good fifteen minutes before the start of her shift. She hadn't even gotten a chance to look up at the assignment board when the charge nurse called her name.

"Serena? Thank God you're here early. Punch in. There's a fresh trauma on the way back from the OR and I don't have anyone to admit her."

She was already swiping her badge as Tess spoke. "What is it?"

"Pedestrian versus car, but the woman was pregnant. They took her for a crash C-section. We've slotted her for bed ten."

Swallowing her dismay, Serena quickly readied the room. Moments later the patient arrived, surrounded by the whole trauma team.

"Get the level-one rapid infuser set up, she's going to need fluids." The trauma surgeon's grim expression made Serena's spirits sink even lower.

She quickly hooked her patient up to the bedside

monitor as the tech ran for the equipment. There wasn't time for a full-blown assessment but she already knew the worst.

The patient was still hemorrhaging badly. Serena opened up all the intravenous fluids to the fullest. "How much blood do we have on hand?"

"There's six units of O-neg here and six more on the way up from the blood bank." The tech wheeled in the equipment and Serena didn't waste any time connecting the lines. Working quickly, she and the tech checked off the blood and primed the infuser.

"What about the baby?" Serena couldn't help but ask.

"The baby didn't make it. The neonatal resuscitation team is bringing the baby in for her husband."

Oh, God. The room spun madly, much like the night she'd admitted Grant. Another stillborn baby.

The alarm from the overhead monitor snagged her attention. Her gaze snapped up. "Blood pressure is down, her heart rate is dropping. She should have enough volume on board. What's her neuro status?"

"Not good before surgery, but we took the chance on being able to save the baby." The trauma resident looked as sick as Serena felt.

Serena pried the woman's eyes open to do a quick neuro exam. Her patient's pupils were fixed and dilated. She flashed the penlight into the woman's eyes again and again, but there was no response.

"Dr. Jerron, you'd better take a look at this."

Serena grabbed the trauma surgeon's arm. "I think I know what's causing her blood pressure problems."

He performed a more comprehensive neuro assessment, checking for other basic reflexes. Then the patient's heart rate dropped further.

"Dammit! I think she's brain dead." The trauma surgeon pounded a fist on the bed. "We didn't think she was stable enough to go to the CT scanner first. I can't believe we're going to lose them both."

Serena glanced up at the monitor again. Her patient's blood pressure continued to drop. Dr. Jerron glanced at the numbers and sighed. "In the OR her blood pressure was going up and up. Now she's crashed. I think she's herniated her brain stem. We'll take her for flows to make sure, but I'll need to prepare her husband for the worst."

Serena continued to titrate the vasopressor medications, although she knew that the situation was hopeless. There was nothing they could do to repair the damage caused by too much swelling of her patient's brain.

The woman's heart rate continued to drop and her blood pressure remained non-existent. Serena almost lost it when the neonatal staff brought the dead infant in with her patient's young husband. The tiny baby looked so much like Daniel she couldn't bear to look. The patient's husband broke into heartfelt sobs, leaning over the bed in an attempt to hold his wife and stillborn child.

Serena silently cried with him. The grim truth hit her hard.

Heroes weren't the only ones who died.

Sometimes the innocent died, too.

CHAPTER NINE

SERENA'S shift didn't get much better. After taking her patient for brain flow studies and finding them non-existent, life support was discontinued. Then, on a more positive note, two other patients were unexpectedly transferred out of ICU. Since she wasn't needed for patient care, she was allowed to leave early. She was grateful to go. In the privacy of her apartment, despair and rage spewed like molten lava from a disturbed volcano.

Unfair! That the mother and child should die was just so unfair. She punched her pillow and cried for the poor husband who'd lost his wife and infant child. Then she cried for herself and the tiny baby she'd buried a year ago.

Slowly her anger ebbed away, leaving a sense of helplessness behind. Still the tears continued to fall. Through her sobs she thought she heard her door buzzer go off downstairs. She ignored the sound. Until there was a loud pounding on her apartment door.

Serena was tempted to ignore that summons, too, but then she remembered Marta and Rico. Sniffling, she wondered if something was wrong. Had Rico taken a turn for the worse? Dragging herself off her bed, she swiped away the signs of her tears the best she could and blew her nose hard before she opened her door.

"Marta? Oh—Grant." She ducked her head, hoping he wouldn't notice her face, blotchy and swollen from crying. She stared at the worn carpeting at his feet. "I...er, wasn't expecting you."

He remained silent and Serena knew he was hoping to be invited in. But she couldn't do it. No way was she in the mood for visitors tonight.

"Serena? What's wrong?" He brushed a damp strand of hair from her cheek. "What has you so upset?"

His quiet kindness was almost too much to bear. She wished he would leave, but at the same time she didn't want to be alone. Her resolve broke. "I— My patient died."

"Come here." He came forward and drew her into his arms, then eased her backward a few steps so he could shut the door behind him. She buried her face in the hollow of his shoulder, muffling her hiccuping sobs against his shirt. Grant didn't seem to mind. He cradled her in his arms and stroked a soothing hand down her back.

"Shh, it's OK. Sometimes that happens. You've been a nurse long enough to know that sometimes patients die."

"She was pregnant. We lost both of them, mom and baby. Her poor husband just stood there and cried." Even now she could still remember the anguish in his voice as he'd told his wife how much he loved her and the kiss he'd bestowed on his dead daughter.

Grant's arms tightened around her as if in understanding. Serena was reminded of those first few days after Eric's death. Grant had held her the same way. He'd been a rock of strength and support. She wouldn't have gotten through Eric's funeral without him.

But for Daniel's funeral, she'd been alone.

"I know, sweetheart, I know. It's OK." He repeated the words over and over until she managed to get herself under control.

She took several deep, calming breaths. Her crying jag was over but she still couldn't seem to make sense of what had happened. "Why? Why did she and the baby have to die?"

"I don't know, sweetheart." He gently reached up to cup Serena's face in his hands. Through her sorrow, her body responded to his touch. Her heart rate quickened when his thumbs stroked her cheek. "I'm sure God has a reason but I just don't know what to tell you."

She turned her face into his hand, pressing her mouth against his palm in a soft kiss. Grant probably hadn't come here tonight just to comfort her, but she'd needed him more than he could ever know.

"Serena," he whispered, turning her face so that he could look at her. She met his gaze, knowing that her need to be with him was clearly reflected in her eyes. His smoky gray eyes darkened with desire. He pulled her insistently closer, giving her plenty of time to back away if she chose to.

Heaven help her, she didn't.

His gaze dropped to her mouth and she eagerly parted her lips in a wordless invitation. As his head bowed toward hers, she met him halfway, claiming his mouth in a mind-numbing kiss.

God, how she'd missed him. His taste was better than the finest champagne and went straight to her head. She melted against him, yearning for more. No man's arms had ever made her feel as safe and secure as Grant's. She silently rejoiced when his mouth plundered hers, his tongue delving deep.

Logical thought fled, replaced by addictive desire. He never let up on the sweet ravishing of her mouth even as she vaguely realized he was steering her down the hall toward her bedroom.

She didn't summon the strength to voice a single protest when he eased her into the bed beside him. His fingers tugged the band out of her ponytail and fanned the silken strands over her shoulders. He buried his face in her hair, inhaling deeply.

Clutching his shoulders, she welcomed every caress, arching her back to mold her breasts more firmly against his chest. Nothing had ever felt this good. His mouth possessed hers again and she met each thrust of his tongue with an eager response of her own. Suddenly, Grant broke off the kiss, his breathing harsh with the effort it took for him to pull away, even for a moment.

"Serena." His voice was thick with desire and he threaded his fingers through her hair. "I need you. Tell me now, if this isn't what you want."

"I— We shouldn't." Helplessly, she stared up at him. She hadn't been intimate with a man since Grant. Had never wanted to. But she needed him now. Her body had instantly come alive under his touch.

"Don't tell me we shouldn't. Tell me what you want." Every muscle in Grant's body was tense, as if bracing himself for her refusal.

"You." She couldn't lie to him, not like this, surrounded by his strong arms and every one of her nerve synapses sparking with anticipation. Slowly, she reached up to unbutton her blouse. He brushed her fingers away and performed the task himself, taking his sweet time.

When he finally finished, Serena arched her back to assist Grant in removing the barrier of her shirt. A deft movement of his hands and her bra followed. He pulled her close. Flesh met flesh and Serena sucked in her breath, drowning in pure sensation. Grant stared down at her, his gaze intense.

A sharp talon of embarrassment stabbed through the haze of passion. Grant looked at her with such an odd expression on his face, she wondered if he'd guess her secret. Had her body changed dramatically from seven months of pregnancy? Would he notice her scar?

For a moment she held her breath, then she cried out as Grant bent his head to take one taut rosy nipple into his mouth, nipping at the bud with his teeth. Serena moved restlessly beneath him, wanting to feel every inch of him against her. Grant must have understood her wordless plea because he yanked open the snap of her jeans and pushed the rough denim down the length of her legs. Serena helped him to remove his as well, taking extra care with the area around his thigh incision. Underclothing followed, until they were both hotly naked against the coolness of the sheets.

The years fell away. When they came together, it was as though they had never been apart. Serena reveled in stroking his chest, the hitch in his breath encouraging her to move her hands lower, then lower still. He groaned when her fist closed around him.

His fingers moved over her, seeking then finding the place she ached to be touched. She bit back a moan. She didn't know where he'd found a condom but she took it out of his hand and put it on him. Grant eased her thighs apart, then covered her mouth with his as he thrust deep, the hardness of his body welcomed by her liquid softness. He groaned against her lips as his hips retreated, then stroked again and again. Serena grasped his shoulders, her legs clamped around his waist as she strained to meet him. Instinctively, her pelvis rotated wildly in response to each thrust.

Serena threw her head back with a wild cry, her

body tightening around him as she met her own release. Grant seemed to hold his breath, staring down at her, watching her come. Then he quickened the pace until, with a gasping cry, he slumped against her. Breathing heavily, he buried his face in the tangled curls of her hair, his massive shoulders shaking with the aftermath of emotion. Serena clung to him, her fingers stroking the corded muscles of his back, reveling in the heaviness of his body against hers.

They stayed like that for a while, each enjoying the closeness of the embrace, until Serena was forced to move or suffocate completely under his weight. Grant sensed her struggle and rolled over. He brought her with him, though, tucking her snugly against him before pulling the covers over the growing coolness of their sweat-dried skin.

Serena reveled in the musky scent of Grant surrounding her. In the aftermath of passion she could face the truth. She hadn't gotten over him in the past eighteen months since their break-up. She hadn't gotten over him at all.

She was still in love with Grant Sullivan.

A muffled cry woke him up hours later, and Grant lifted his head from the pillow on Serena's bed where they'd both fallen asleep.

He pushed himself to his elbows, glancing wildly around the room, his cop instincts sensing something amiss. Within moments, he realized that the source of the noise was Serena. She thrashed on the bed.

"No, please, don't die. Daniel…" The sheer anguish in her voice squeezed his heart.

He reached for her. "Serena—dear God, Serena wake up."

Her arms flailed wildly against him. She jerked from his touch, frantically pushing the covers aside as if searching for something beneath the folds. Grant tried to calm her down, but the throes of the nightmare held her captive.

"Daniel…no, don't die."

"Serena, I'm here. You're safe now, sweetheart." Grant dodged her pummeling arms and pulled her against the solid wall of his chest, praying she would wake up soon. She stopped fighting, burrowing her face into his shoulder. He continued to talk soothingly, hoping to reach her subconscious. Grant held her tight, shaken at the sight of her tear-stained face pulled into an agonizing mask of pain. She kept sobbing the name Daniel over and over again, even as she hung onto him with a vise-like grip.

Grant rocked her back and forth, smoothing a hand over her long, unbound hair. Slowly Serena's sobs trailed away to a few uneven breaths as she let go of the last vestiges of her nightmare.

His body instantly reacted to the way Serena pressed her bare body against his chest. With a grimace, he acknowledged the bad timing and ignored his body's basic instinct. Apparently her nightmare had passed but, loath as he was to disturb her, there was a burning question he just couldn't ignore.

"Who's Daniel?"

Immediately, every muscle in her body tensed and a horrible sense of dread settled in his gut. Here was her secret. Was there a man in her life after all? Someone with whom she planned to share her future? Dear God, another death she'd been forced to deal with?

"Our son."

Grant blinked. No, that couldn't be right. He must have heard wrong. Grasping her shoulders, he eased her away, staring down at her damp face and tangled red-gold hair. He could barely see her distraught facial features in the early dawn light. "What did you say?"

Serena dropped her gaze guiltily from his. "Our son. When we broke off our engagement, I discovered I was pregnant."

"Pregnant?" He swept his gaze over her body, looking for any signs that she'd borne a child. His hand dropped down to her stomach and he smoothed his hand over the soft curve, feeling the slight indentation of a scar. Had she miscarried? Or had she given the child away? Panic clutched him, even though he knew Serena well enough to know she wouldn't have given their child away.

Would she?

He braced himself. "What happened?"

"During my seventh month, I went into labor unexpectedly. They gave me medication to stop the labor but the baby's heart rate dropped. They did an emergency C-section, but it was too late. He… Daniel was stillborn.''

There was a strained silence. Grant struggled to grasp the concept. He'd had a son who'd died? For a moment the picture of Ben flashed into his mind and he felt a piercing pain in the region of his heart. A child. A baby. He'd always wanted a son. Or a daughter.

He could barely force the question past vocal cords gone frozen. ''Why didn't you tell me?''

She drew a deep breath and let it out slowly. The flash of guilt in her eyes told him she knew there wasn't a good reason for her to keep such a secret. ''I didn't want you to come back, just for the sake of the baby.''

''I'd say that was a pretty damn good reason.'' Grant drew away from her, stifling the urge to smack his hand against the mattress. There wasn't anything he could do now but, dammit, she'd hidden the truth from him. ''A son. You should have told me, Serena. I had a right to know.''

''Would it have made a difference?'' She tilted her chin, silently challenging him now. ''Tell me the truth, Grant. Would knowing about your son have changed your mind about quitting the force?''

''No.'' He climbed out of bed and reached for his discarded boxer shorts. Pulling them on, he raked a hand through his hair and let out a harsh laugh. ''Knowing about our son wouldn't have made me quit the force, Serena.''

"See? That's why I didn't tell you." Her eyes were twin blue pools of despair. He steeled himself against her imploring gaze.

"Don't you get it? I'm a cop. I'll live, breathe and die a cop. There isn't anything in the world that can change that."

"Why?" Anguish filled her voice. Fresh tears glistened in her eyes. "Why, Grant?"

"Do you realize that's the first time you've ever asked me that?" He crossed over to her bedroom window, turning the blinds to allow additional early morning light in because he didn't trust himself to be near her. A lie of this magnitude would be difficult to forgive. But when Serena filled his arms, his common sense took flight. He'd likely forgive her anything. Especially if she'd give him a second chance. All of him. Including the career that was so much a part of him.

Serena sniffled loudly. "No, I didn't realize that. If I didn't ask before, I'm asking now. Why is being a cop so important to you?"

He didn't know if he could make her understand, but he was willing to try. Although even after all this time, talking about the incident still pained him. "You know my sister Cheryl is four years younger than me." She nodded and he continued, "when you're eleven there's nothing worse than having a little sister tagging along, being a pest. Mom used to make me take her with me when I met my friends at the park, telling me to keep an eye on her."

"Younger sisters can be a hassle sometimes." Serena's expression turned wistful and he suspected she was remembering her relationship with Eric.

He sighed. "I resented having to bring her along, so one day I ditched her. The park was only two blocks from our house. I figured she'd go crying home to Mom, but at least I could ride off with my friends without worrying about her keeping up. To me the risk of punishment was worth being alone with my friends."

"What happened?"

"She didn't come home." Even now, the memory of what he'd done grabbed him by the throat. "Hours later, my dad tracked me down at my buddy's house after he combed the park looking for us. But Cherrie was gone. I never saw my parents so upset. I knew it was my fault, but they didn't yell and scream at me. They did call the police. Two cops showed up on our doorstep and they took me back to the park, made me go over exactly where I'd left her."

"Oh, no. How awful. But, Grant, you were just a child yourself."

"Old enough to know better." He'd learned to live with the decision that had changed his life. But she hadn't heard the worst yet. "I didn't know that there had been another child abduction in the park, just the day before. Somehow the cops had kept that tidbit of information from hitting the media. They thought for sure the same guy had grabbed my sister."

Serena sucked in a harsh breath.

He raised tortured eyes to hers. "You have no idea what we went through during the hours they searched. They found her about midnight. Thank God she hadn't been taken after all, but had gotten completely lost. She'd cried and wandered around the park, looking for our house. When those cops brought her home, safe and unharmed, my parents wept with relief. Even my dad. I don't think I ever saw him cry except that once."

He noticed Serena was struggling not to cry again herself but she didn't interrupt.

"When I saw that officer carrying Cheryl in his arms with a big grin on his face, I knew I'd be a cop just like him one day. I suppose it sounds stupid, but I always felt as if I needed to dedicate my life to serving the public, as if I could atone for my mistake."

She drew a long ragged breath. "No, it doesn't sound stupid at all."

Grant stared down at the carpet for a minute. "So, you see, nothing will change my mind about my career, Serena. Not even knowing you were pregnant with my child. Guys like me protect the innocent. Just like that cop protected Cherrie." He swallowed hard and raised his gaze to hers. "Does our son have a grave?"

The resigned look in her eyes told him she finally accepted the truth. "Yes. It's located in the small cemetery behind my church."

"I'd like to see it."

She nodded. "I'll show you. I hope you don't mind, but I christened him Daniel Eric."

He stared at her for a long time wishing for something that could never be. "The only thing I mind is that his last name wasn't Sullivan."

CHAPTER TEN

SERENA couldn't force a response from her constricted throat. Grant left her bedroom, the door closing behind him with a loud click. She buried her face in her hands.

Dear God, what had she done? Grant deserved to know the truth, but now he'd never forgive her lie. Not that she could completely blame him. Would she have told him the truth if Daniel had lived? She'd like to think so.

Scrambling to her feet, she searched for her clothes. Maybe she better understood Grant's dedication to his career but she couldn't change her fear of him dying a hero. Like he nearly had the night she'd worked in the trauma room. Why couldn't he understand that? Or didn't he even want to try?

Intent on finding him, she opened her bedroom door then froze. The door across the hall was open. Grant stood inside her spare bedroom, gazing around. As always, the room pulled at her and she crossed the threshold. A wave of sadness crushed her chest despite being surrounded by the cheery yellow walls decorated with a Noah's Ark border complete with dancing pairs of animals. Against her will her feet took a familiar path. She brushed past Grant and settled in the rocker, facing the empty crib.

"Why haven't you cleaned out this room, Serena?" he asked, his voice gruff.

She rocked in the chair, back and forth, back and forth. Her eyes remained trained on the empty crib. "I can't."

"Serena." Grant placed a hand on her chair, halting her hypnotic motion. "This isn't healthy."

Swallowing hard, she nodded. "I know. At first I spent hours in here, day after day. Then I realized I needed help. I was severely depressed and I went into counseling, even took anti-depressants. I've been better these past few months. My doctor weaned me off the medication. I've even discussed dismantling this room, donating everything to charity."

"Then why haven't you?"

"I don't know. I just can't. There's a part of me that feels like Daniel will really be gone for ever if I take everything out of his room." She knew none of this made any sense, but there was no help for it. None of her feelings made sense, not regarding Daniel's room, not Grant's career.

But how did anyone change a basic part of their nature?

"So this is why you were so upset last night." Grant drew her up and out of the chair. She wanted to stay in the rocker but forced herself to stand. He tipped her chin, forcing her to meet his gaze. "The mother and the baby dying was too much."

"No." She shook her head, pulling away from his touch. "I mean, yes, of course. But not just that. More the realization that if I had died with Daniel, there wouldn't have been any husband to cry at my bedside."

"Serena, what am I going to do with you?" He crushed her in his arms and held her close. "If I had known about the baby, I would have been there. You know that, don't you? I would have been there for you. For our son."

"I know." She pulled away and steeled her resolve to look around the room one last time. Seeing the room through Grant's eyes, she noticed the thick layer of dust that coated the furniture. The dismal sight of waste. Some other child could be enjoying these things. Some young mother who couldn't afford to buy things for herself. She risked a glance at him. "I know I should have given you that chance."

He didn't actually agree, but she figured he was thinking the same thing.

Although it was difficult, she walked across the room toward the door. "Let's get something to eat."

"Sounds good." Grant followed her out and closed the door behind him. "You know, I'll help you with this room when you're ready to tackle it."

"Thanks." Serena was surprised by his offer. Would she be able to dismantle the room if Grant was with her? Maybe. She took a deep breath and nodded. "Yeah. I just might take you up on that."

"First, though, I'll make breakfast." Grant rubbed his stomach. "My appetite has finally returned."

"Glad to hear it." Serena ran a hand through her tousled hair. "I'd rather take a quick shower first."

"Take your time. Culinary creations need patience. These things can't be rushed."

Rolling her eyes, she headed for the bathroom. While Serena showered, Grant rummaged through cupboards to find the necessary food and utensils. Whistling through his teeth, he cracked eggs in a bowl to make omelets.

The eggs were sizzling in the pan when he heard Serena coming out of her bedroom. A knock at the door had him glancing at her in surprise.

"Don't you have to buzz to get in?"

"You managed last night, you know." Serena headed for the door. "Besides, this could be Marta."

"Serena?" Marta's pretty face was pinched with worry. A somber, multi-bruised Rico stood beside her. "The Department of Social Services is coming this afternoon. I need your help."

"Of course." Serena gestured for the pair to come in. Grant turned down the heat beneath the fry pan and came toward them. "Oh, Marta and Rico, this is Grant Sullivan. Grant, my neighbors across the hall, Marta and her younger brother, Rico."

"Pleased to meet you." Grant held out his hand to Marta, then to Rico. He wondered what the hell had happened to the kid, but held his curiosity in check. After a moment's hesitation, the boy gripped his hand with a firm grasp. He grinned at the kid with approval. "Are you guys hungry? I'm making omelets."

"Er…no, that's OK." Marta seemed nervous around him, though he didn't know why. Rico dropped his gaze to the floor. "Serena, would you mind coming over about one? That's when the social worker is due to arrive."

"Sure thing. I think we should let them know how I help you keep an eye on Rico." Serena gave the younger woman's hand a quick squeeze. "Don't worry, Marta. We'll do our best to make this work."

"Thank you, Serena. I don't know what I'd do without you." Marta smiled at Grant, although her smile didn't reach her eyes. "Nice meeting you. See you later, Serena."

The pair left and Grant turned back to his cooking. But the questions wouldn't leave him alone. Marta seemed awfully young to have custody of a child Rico's age. And what was up with the boy? Who had worked the poor kid over?

He slid one omelet on a plate and handed it to Serena. Then he scooped the second one for himself. Seated across the table, Serena dug into her food with more gusto than he'd have believed an hour ago.

"So, what was that all about?" He tried to keep his tone casual, but curiosity was killing him.

She shrugged. "Nothing much. Marta is having a tough time. She's Rico's sister and legal guardian. I'm trying to help out."

"What happened to Rico?"

"He got himself mixed up with the Hombres."
Serena shook her head with a sigh. "They beat him
up, though I'm not sure why. Maybe because he was
trying to cut loose."

"The Hombres?" Grant's fork clattered to his
plate. "Good God, Serena, the Hombres are killing
cops for initiation rites. What if Rico was involved
the night I was shot?"

Serena's shoulders tensed and she glared at him,
clearly upset with his accusing tone. "Rico isn't a
killer, Grant. I don't think he'd been initiated as a
member yet. But if what you say is true, then he's
lucky to get away with a beating. What if they go
after him with guns instead of fists?"

"Hell, Serena, you don't know if the kid was involved or not. But if he knows some of the gang
members, this might be our lucky break. I need to
call the captain."

"No, you don't." Serena jumped up as he rose
from his seat. "Grant, for heaven's sake. Give me
some time before you jump on this. Marta is a wreck.
After Rico was attacked, they pretty much treated her
as if she were some sort of child abuser. Social
Services is coming here in…" she glanced at her
watch "…three hours. Don't you think that's enough
stress for now?"

"OK, I'll give you some time. But after this little
meeting is over, you'd better let me talk to Rico.
Tomorrow at the latest. Hell, Serena, another cop's
life could be at stake."

She hesitated, then reluctantly nodded. He wanted to leap into action, but understood that co-operation was key. First let Marta and Rico get through this little visit. Then he'd get his time with the boy to grill him for information.

Grant carried his dirty dishes to the sink. After he'd gotten some information to go on, there was a chance the captain would let him assist on the case. He couldn't do fieldwork, but he could sure as heck sit behind a desk.

Not until he'd gotten halfway home did Grant remember his promise to help Serena with Daniel's room.

Serena met with Marta and Rico fifteen minutes before the social worker was due to arrive. Marta had taken the day off and was putting together some snacks in the kitchen. In the living room, Rico sat quietly, his dark eyes full of apprehension.

"What's the matter, Rico?" Serena dropped onto a threadbare sofa beside him.

"Nuthin'." He shrugged one shoulder.

"Are you worried about being taken away from Marta?" Serena figured there was no reason to dance around the crux of the matter.

"Maybe."

She suppressed a sigh. His one-word answers were getting to her. "Why did those boys attack you?"

"I dunno." He picked at a stray thread on the cushion of the couch.

Serena suspected he did know but, short of tying him up by his toenails and torturing the truth out of him, she couldn't force him to confide in her. She decided not to mention Grant's desire to talk to him about the Hombres. Time enough for the police to be involved after the social worker's visit.

Exactly at one the buzzer sounded. Marta wrung her hands as she pushed the button to allow the woman to come up. Serena wished there were something more she could do to put her friend at ease.

Marta opened the door.

"Ms. Gonzales?" A middle-aged woman with dark hair sprinkled with gray greeted her.

Marta mutely nodded.

"I'm Ms. Stilman, the social worker assigned to your case. May I come in?"

Overall, Serena felt the visit went well. Ms. Stilman had several pointed questions for Marta, then she also pinned Rico on his relationship with the Hombres.

"I don't hang with them any more," he told her.

Understandably, Ms. Stilman didn't seem convinced. "What happens the next time you're home alone and they show up? How are you going to resist the lure of their friendship?"

Rico hadn't come up with a great answer for that one, other than to reinforce that he wasn't going to hang with them any more. Ms. Stilman requested a copy of Marta's work schedules for the two jobs she held.

"I live across the hall and help keep an eye on

Rico when Marta is working." She glanced at Rico, who caught on quickly and nodded. "Just the other day, he came over for breakfast. And there's a program at Trinity that I'm recommending for Marta. If she could get a full-time job there, the hospital will pay for her to go to nursing school. She's looking into the program."

"Really?" Ms. Stilman appeared impressed with that information. "I think that would be a great idea. There's a huge nursing shortage now."

After a grueling hour of questions and a brief tour of Marta's apartment, including Rico's bedroom, Ms. Stilman seemed satisfied.

"Well, I think things can remain the way they are for now. But if Rico gets himself into trouble again, I'm afraid we'll be forced to take a stronger stance."

"But the fact that he was assaulted isn't his fault," Marta protested.

"Except he's admitted to hanging with the Hombres, which is trouble. And his fault." Ms. Stilman softened her words with a smile. "But it seems as if he's trying to get his life back on track. I'm glad to see you're taking his welfare seriously, Marta."

Marta put her arm around Rico's shoulders. "We're family. We'll be fine."

"Good. I really hope that's true." Ms. Stilman turned to Serena. "Ms. Mitchell. Nice to meet you. Marta and Rico, call me if you need anything, OK?"

Rico let out a big sigh when Ms. Stilman left. "Whew. I didn't think she was ever gonna leave."

"You heard her, Rico. You must stay away from those Hombres. If you don't, they'll take you away." Marta was back to wringing her hands.

"Hey, I thought the visit went well." Serena made an effort to lighten Marta's sour mood. "She's really on your side, Marta. I think your dedication to Rico and to providing a stable home for him really helped."

"*Gracias*, Serena. Thanks for your help."

Serena cleared her throat. "You're welcome but I need a favor, too. Rico, remember earlier this morning when you met Grant Sullivan?" He nodded and she continued, "He's a cop. He'd like to talk to you about the Hombres."

Rico's eyes widened in alarm and he backed up several steps. "No! I know nothing."

"You know they're shooting cops, don't you?" Serena persisted. "Grant was not long ago. Did you know that? They think the Hombres are responsible."

He shrank against Marta. "I can't tell. I can't!"

"Listen, Rico. Those boys are trouble. If they get arrested, they can't hurt you any more, right?" Marta took him by the shoulders and pierced him with her gaze. "This is important. If you do this, the social worker will really know you plan to stay away from them for good."

Indecision clouded his eyes. Finally he nodded, although his chin dragged on his chest. "OK. I'll go."

''Thank you, Rico.'' Serena squeezed his shoulder. ''I know this isn't easy, but anything, even the smallest detail, might help.''

Marta nodded her agreement. ''When do you need him?''

''Now, if that's all right.'' Serena glanced at her watch. Grant probably wasn't expecting them this early but she was worried that, given additional time to think about this, Rico could change his mind. ''I'll drive.''

Rico huddled in the corner of her car's passenger seat, withdrawing into silence. Serena didn't know what to say to make this easier for him. She knew he felt as if he were ratting on his friends, but what sort of friends beat you up when you didn't want to hang around any more?

Luckily, the ride to Grant's bungalow was a short one. She pulled up to the curb, glancing through her window to make sure his rusted Chevy was parked in the driveway.

There was a chocolate brown Grand Am parked in the driveway instead. As she watched, the passenger door opened and a brown-haired boy tumbled out. Grant stood in the doorway and laughingly scooped up the boy when the kid launched himself at him. A beautiful brunette stepped out of the driver's side.

''Ben, take it easy! Don't hurt Grant's stitches!''

''Ah, don't worry, slugger.'' Grant's grin from ear to ear clearly showed he didn't mind. ''Ben just missed me, didn't you? Well you know what? I missed you, too.''

''Are you gonna come to my Little League game tomorrow night?'' Ben wanted to know.

''Ben,'' Loren warned. ''Don't start.''

''Of course I'll be there.'' Grant propped open his door, a silent invitation for Loren to come inside. ''Wouldn't miss it for the world.''

Frozen, Serena stared at the image the three of them made as a picture-perfect family. They disappeared inside Grant's house and she didn't move. She couldn't breathe, couldn't hear or feel a thing.

Grant hadn't missed Daniel. The knowledge slammed into her chest with the force of a blow. Not in the same way she had mourned the loss of her son. Grant had kept his career, and he'd also found his own ready-made family with Loren and Ben.

Serena's chest burned with the effort it took to breathe. Thousands of glass shards replaced the oxygen in her lungs. Watching Grant with Ben was worse than painful. Grant obviously had a relationship with Ben, one he'd never have with Daniel.

His own son.

CHAPTER ELEVEN

GRANT enjoyed goofing around with Ben, although his incisions ached abominably when the boy tried to tackle him. Finally Loren called a halt to the torture.

"Ben, run out to the car to get my purse," Loren directed.

"Aw, Mom. Do I hav'ta?"

"Yes. Please."

After rolling his eyes dramatically, the boy dashed outside. Loren let out a heavy sigh. "Sorry about that. Are you OK?"

He grimaced and rubbed a hand over his chest. "I'll survive."

"So, I stopped by to see you last night after my shift." Loren pushed the toe of her running shoe into the pile of his carpet, eyes downcast. "You weren't home."

Warning bells jangled in his head. Loren had stopped by? At midnight last night? Grant knew he'd been with Serena. Her scent was still imbedded in his senses. Guilt weighed heavily on his shoulders. Loren deserved to know the truth.

"No, I wasn't." Desperate, he searched for the right way to tell her the truth without hurting her feelings. "You know I'll always be here for you and Ben.

But I have to be honest with you, Loren. I recently discovered I'm still in love with my ex-fiancée.''

"I see." She kept her gaze on the floor, as if the pattern in his gray carpet was enthralling. "I wondered. Who is she?"

Man, he didn't like hurting her like this. "Loren, I'm sorry if I misled you in any way. You and Ben have been wonderful for me. You helped me see what is really important in life." His smile was crooked. "You're actually the perfect woman for me. But my heart won't listen to my head."

"You didn't answer my question, Grant. Who is she?"

"Serena Mitchell. She's a trauma critical care nurse at Trinity Medical Center."

A ghost of a smile flittered over her features. "A nurse, huh? Too bad, because it just so happens I think you're the perfect man for us, especially for Ben."

He noted how she included her son in the deal. Was it possible Loren's feelings were also dependent on his relationship with her son? If he hadn't been good father material for Ben, would she have walked away? The thought eased his swirling discomfort. "Hey, Ben is an awesome kid. Some day you'll fall in love with a guy who will also be a good father for Ben. Don't sell yourself short, Loren. You deserve to be happy."

"Yeah, but the dating scene isn't really my thing." She shrugged, then turned toward the door. "Well, I guess we should get going. Don't feel obligated to come to Ben's game. He probably shouldn't depend on you so much.''

The thought of breaking his promise to Ben didn't sit well with Grant. Ben didn't deserve to be left out in the cold just because Grant didn't love his mother. Losing his father hadn't been Ben's fault. Which was exactly what Serena had been worried about. If Daniel had lived, and Grant had died in the trauma room that night, his son would be just like Ben, growing up without a father.

''I'll be there. You can count on it.'' Grant refused to let the kid down. Having a mom at Little League wasn't exactly the same as having a father figure watch you play.

''Well, just so you know, I won't hold you to it.'' Loren glanced away as Ben rushed back inside.

''I can't find your purse, Mom,'' he complained. ''I looked under the seats and everything.''

''Oh, that's right. I brought it in with me.'' She pulled it out of the corner of the sofa as if surprised to see she'd had it all along. The smile on her face didn't reach her eyes. ''Sorry about that, Ben. Say goodbye to Grant. We need to get going.''

''Bye, Grant. See you tomorrow.'' Ben cheerfully gave Grant a big hug.

''I'll be there.'' Grant returned the boy's embrace, holding the tiny body tight. So sturdy, yet so fragile. If anything ever happened to Ben… He couldn't finish the thought. Serena's fears suddenly didn't seem quite so irrational. Maybe he could make some sort of compromise with her. If he'd been wearing his body armor, his injuries would have been minor. Maybe if he promised to wear his flak jacket religiously, she'd give him another chance.

Grant watched Loren and Ben buckle up in Loren's car, then slowly drive away. How on earth had Serena buried their son all alone?

And how did a parent ever get over the loss of their child?

After checking his watch for the third time in ten minutes, Grant reached for the phone. He'd asked Serena to give him a chance to talk to Rico. What on earth was taking the social worker's visit so long? He hoped there weren't problems. But he wouldn't know unless he asked.

Serena's phone rang, then her answering-machine picked up. He left a terse message, then hung up. Bored and restless, he paced the small expanse of his living room. Sure, he wanted to talk to Rico, but underneath he knew he really just wanted to see Serena again. The images from last night's love-making teased his senses, stirring the embers of dormant desire. He was glad Loren knew the truth, even if admitting he still loved Serena had been difficult. Doubts assailed him. Did Serena feel even remotely the same? Or was she right now remembering all the reasons she'd walked away before?

Within minutes, his phone rang again. He pounced. "Serena?"

There was a long pause. "Hell, no, this isn't Serena." The captain's caustic voice crackled over the line. "Is that how you answer your damn phone?"

"No, sorry about that, Captain." Grant rubbed the tense muscles along the back of his neck. "What's up?"

"Just wanted to thank you for sending Serena and Rico in to talk to us." He could hear the captain chewing what was, no doubt, another antacid, in his ear. "Rico didn't have a lot of information to share, but we have a few new leads to follow up on."

Puzzled, Grant sank onto the edge of his sofa. "Serena brought Rico in to see you? Why?"

"I figured her coming in to see us was your idea. Wasn't it?"

"Uh, yeah. Sort of." What in the heck had Serena done? Purposefully gone behind his back to make sure he wasn't involved in this case? He could hardly believe what the captain was telling him. He strove to keep his tone normal. "I'm glad you got some leads out of the deal."

"Sullivan, you weren't planning on talking to the boy yourself, were you?" The captain's voice took on a hard edge. "I warned you about meddling in this case. Thank God Serena doesn't listen to you."

His face flamed, and he was thankful the captain couldn't see his guilty reaction. "What kinds of leads did he give you? Names of other gang members? Details of their initiation rites? What?"

"Hah! Caught you in the act." The captain

sounded positively gleeful. "You are trying to work this case. I'll slap a discipline in your file, see if I don't!"

"Fine. Whatever." Grant scowled at the phone. "Is that all you wanted to tell me?"

"That, and to keep your nose out of my case." The captain hung up in his ear.

Grant lay back on the sofa, wincing as the muscles in his chest pulled. He called Serena again, but there was still no answer. Had she stayed with Rico and Marta? Was she at work? He always had trouble keeping her work schedule straight. For all he knew, she could be working any day, any shift.

With a sigh, he closed his eyes. Serena had gone over his head, straight to the captain. Did she really resent his career that much? Why hadn't she come to see him herself, even without Rico? Was she already regretting their time together?

With a sinking sensation in the pit of his stomach, Grant vowed to force Serena to listen to his new resolution. Surely she owed him that much at least?

Serena and Rico spent several hours down at the third district Milwaukee Police station, talking about the Hombres with Captain Reichert. At first Serena had to pry each bit of information out of Rico, step by step. But toward the end words tumbled from his lips, as if the horrible deeds were purulent fluid he needed to drain from his soul.

Afterwards, Serena drove Rico home. Marta

seemed calmer and informed Serena that she'd applied for a job in the food-service department at Trinity Medical Center, using Serena's name as a reference. Relieved that Marta was taking steps in the right direction, she gave the woman a hug.

"I'm so glad. They'll call to offer you a job, you'll see."

Alone in her apartment, Serena thought about Grant. She flipped the answering-machine on so she wouldn't have to take his calls. Then she wandered down the hall to Daniel's room.

As always, when she approached the door, her stomach cramped painfully. Imaginary pains, but real enough deep in her heart. For a moment her hand hovered over the doorknob. Grant had offered to help her dismantle the room. Should she call him?

Remembering the way he'd greeted Ben, his face alight with laughter, firmed her resolve. No one had been closer to her child than she had been. She'd clean out Daniel's room and put him to rest once and for all.

She squared her shoulders and pushed open the door. The yellow, dusty walls didn't look nearly as inviting now that she'd seen the room through Grant's eyes. Full of determination, she went straight to the crib and stripped the dust-lined baby linen from the bed. Then she took the mattress out and propped it against the wall. Eyeing the frame of the crib, she realized she needed a screwdriver. Before she could change her mind, she went in search of her mini-toolbox and brought the tools into the room.

She could do this. There was no reason at all for her to call Grant.

When the phone rang a while later, and she heard his voice on her answering-machine, she ignored his call.

With loving care, she packed the last of Daniel's things in a cardboard box, dampened with tears.

By the next day, she was tired of dodging Grant. He'd come to see her several times. As an escape she called Trinity to see if they needed any help. She quickly agreed to work the evening shift. Anything to get away from Grant, to avoid hearing his explanations about Loren and Ben.

"Hey, Serena, thanks for coming in." Marion, the evening shift charge nurse, greeted her with a grateful smile. "Your patient assignment is pretty easy, a simple vascular surgery patient who should have gone out today except for the fact that his heart showed some suspicious EKG changes indicative of a myocardial infarction. The second patient is a liver transplant who is doing very well and should also go out to the general floor tomorrow."

"Great." Serena almost wished she had a busier assignment, to keep her mind from dwelling on Grant. "I'll get a report."

The first shift nurse gave Serena a report on both patients, then left. When she entered the first patient's room she was pleasantly surprised to find Mr. Eichstadt awake.

"Hello, Mr. Eichstadt. My name is Serena and I'm your evening shift nurse. How are you feeling? Are you having any pain?"

"Nah, the pain isn't too bad. I'm doing fine. Except I'm waiting for my wife. She told me she was coming in today."

"Hmm." Serena subtly checked his vitals from the monitor above his head, making notations on her clipboard. "Would you like me to call her for you?"

"When you have time."

"Serena?" She turned to glance at the doorway. One of her peers stood there, holding up a phone receiver. "Is Mr. Eichstadt able to have visitors? His wife is here."

"Absolutely. Send her in." Serena turned back to her patient with a smile. "Your wife is already here, Mr. Eichstadt. She'll be up shortly."

"Oh, good. I was afraid something had happened to her." The elderly gentleman appeared relieved. "I don't like her driving back and forth so much."

"I can understand. I'm going to take a peek at your incisions." Serena lifted the sheets. Everything looked fine. His heart rhythm was still a bit irregular and every few minutes he had a long pause between heartbeats, but otherwise he looked good. Probably he could have been monitored on a telemetry unit if his doctor hadn't been so conservative.

"Hello? Someone told me I could come in."

Serena gestured for the woman to enter the room. "Mrs. Eichstadt, my name is Serena and I'm your husband's nurse. He's been waiting anxiously for you to arrive."

"Oh, Edgar." The tiny, spry white-haired woman leaned over the bed rail to plant a kiss on her husband's cheek. "I promised to come around four, didn't I? Did you think I'd miss our fiftieth anniversary?"

"Your fiftieth? I'm so impressed! Congratulations." This was the part of nursing she sometimes missed, having patients who could converse. Critical-care nursing was interesting and demanding, but more often than not her patients couldn't talk.

"Thank you. Fifty years. We've been very blessed." Mrs. Eichstadt pulled up a chair and settled next to her husband's bed. He reached over and took her hand in his.

"Sure, she says that now. Remember those early years?" The older man teased.

Mrs. Eichstadt rolled her eyes. "Yes, those years you were with the Marines were awful. I absolutely hated all that moving around." She glanced at Serena with a wry smile. "I was so painfully shy back then. Every time we'd pick up and move I'd be surrounded by all these new people that I couldn't find the courage to talk to. Edgar made friends easily, he never seemed to mind. And once our first child was born, my housebound days grew longer. I swear there were times I worried about my sanity.''

''Did Mr. Eichstadt get out of the Marines after his first tour?'' Serena asked, curious how this couple managed to make a marriage work for fifty years.

''Gosh, no!'' Mrs. Eichstadt laughed. ''Edgar loved being a Marine. I knew he was in the service when we married, so I learned to live with the stress of moving from location to location.''

''Wow. That must have been difficult.'' Serena frowned. Why did women always have to be the ones to give in? She would have figured that Mr. Eichstadt would have gotten out of the Marines to make his wife happy.

''Well, yes, learning to live with the frequent moves was difficult,'' Mrs. Eichstadt confessed. ''But, then, marriage is difficult in other ways, too.'' She beamed at her husband. ''When you love someone, it's worth the effort it takes to make a relationship work.''

Serena nodded, and turned to check on her second patient. When that was finished, she secretly called down to the kitchen, asking for a special cake to be brought up to the ICU as a surprise anniversary celebration for the Eichstadts. Then she rallied some of her fellow nurses to go in with her to present the cake.

The Eichstadts were thrilled with the small surprise. Mr. Eichstadt was supposed to be limited to taking clear liquids, but Serena had gotten the OK from the doctor to give him at least one bite of cake. Hopefully, his stomach wouldn't revolt.

Everyone clapped when Mrs. Eichstadt kissed her husband on the mouth, smearing frosting on his face. Serena watched the couple in awe.

Mrs. Eichstadt's parting words stayed with her for a long time. *When you love someone, it's worth the effort it takes to make the relationship work.*

Moving from place to place was very different than the scenario she faced with Grant. He put his life on the line every day. But, then, Mrs. Eichstadt mentioned fearing for her sanity. The couple had survived fifty years together.

Had she honestly given her relationship with Grant her best effort?

Serena's shift was nearing the end when one of her co-workers came to find her. "Serena? There's a boy named Rico down in the emergency department. He's asking for you."

Rico? Had he been assaulted again? Serena rushed for the phone. "Rico? What happened? Are you all right?"

"Come down, Serena. Marta's hurt."

"I'll be right there. Don't move." Serena slammed down the phone. "Emma? Will you cover my patients for me? My neighbor is downstairs in the ED and her twelve-year-old brother is down there alone."

"Of course. Holler if you need help."

Serena nodded and dashed out of the unit. She took

the nearest stairwell to the main floor, then headed straight for the emergency department. She couldn't imagine what had happened to Marta. Some sort of accident? Had she fallen down the stairs?

Using her ID badge, she gained access to the emergency department. Glancing at the huge whiteboard on one wall, she identified Marta's room.

Rico was waiting for her. The minute he saw her, he threw himself into her arms.

"My fault, this is my fault." He sobbed, his skinny arms clamped around her waist. "They got her."

"Who got her?" Serena clutched Rico close, but her gaze found Marta lying on the gurney. She'd been badly beaten, just like Rico had been. Marta's bruised face caused dread to congeal into desperate fear. "The Hombres?" Serena gasped. "Dear God, the Hombres did this to her?"

"Because of me." She was shocked at Rico's revelation, but before she could reassure him he broke free. "Stay with Marta. I'm going to get them. I know where they are."

"What? No, Rico, wait." Serena grabbed for his arm, but missed. The boy darted off. Serena cast a helpless glance at Marta, then followed Rico. "Rico! Wait for me!"

The kid was fast. He also knew exactly where he was going. Dodging emergency department equipment and busy personnel, he took a path straight for the doors.

"Stop him! Rico!" Serena kept after him, but he

sprinted outside with all the energy of youth. Serena made it to the doors a few minutes later, but even as she wildly glanced around he was nowhere to be found.

"Rico!" Panting, Serena propped one arm on the brick wall. Where were the Hombres now? Two days ago, Rico had told the police the Hombres often moved between several locations.

She needed help fast. Then she saw Rico again. Nothing more than the brief outline of his small frame, silhouetted against the light from the parking lot. Suddenly she remembered one of the sites Rico had mentioned was the park across from the middle school.

She ducked inside the ED. "Here, call upstairs to the ICU, tell Emma she needs to take over my patient assignment. Then call this number." She scribbled Grant's number on a slip of paper. "Tell Grant to meet me at the park a few blocks down from Parkway Middle School. Tell him Rico's in trouble with the Hombres."

Shoving the paper at the stunned unit secretary, Serena left. Now that she knew where Rico was going, she prayed she wouldn't be too late.

CHAPTER TWELVE

GRANT had gotten home a few hours earlier from visiting Daniel's grave and was brooding about fatherhood when the phone rang. He had trouble figuring out what the woman from Trinity Medical was trying to tell him. Then his blood ran cold. Marta had been badly beaten. Serena had taken off after Rico, who was going after the Hombres for hurting his sister.

He grabbed his weapon and flung himself to the driver's seat of his battered, rusty Chevy. With one hand he dialed the MPD on his cellphone as he headed for the park.

''There is possible gang activity in the park across from Parkway Middle School,'' Grant informed the dispatcher. ''Requesting back-up. Notify Captain Reichert. He'll want to get some men out there, a.s.a.p.''

He parked his car alongside a portion of the road overhung with trees and lined with brush. Gun in hand, he crept from his car. There wasn't much light from the moon, but there were a few scattered streetlights still working. Several others had lamps that were broken, no doubt by the gang members.

The hair on his neck rose in alarm. He was reminded of the night he'd found the dead rookie lying

in a bloody puddle in the center of the street. Using
the bushes for cover, he swept his gaze over the area,
alert for any movement. Where in the hell were Rico
and Serena?

As he rounded the corner of the bushes he noticed
an outbuilding located off in one corner of the park.
He stared at the structure. Had he seen movement?
Were they behind the building, shielded from view of
the road? There wasn't much cover between the
bushes where he was hidden and the structure. If the
kids were there, deep in the shadows, they might see
him before he reached them.

Grant took a deep breath. He couldn't wait. His
best approach would be to take them by surprise.
Were they armed? With a sense of defeat, he realized
he'd left without his flak jacket.

Again.

Mentally preparing for the worst, he took a deep
breath, then ran. The building was only about two
hundred yards away, but with pain shooting down his
injured thigh, the distance seemed endless.

As he grew closer, he saw the group of kids,
dressed in dark green to blend with the night. There
was a woman—dear God, Serena—standing with her
hands up as if in surrender. Rico stood off to her left.
The pack of kids stood threateningly and, from what
Grant could tell, at least one kid standing in front of
the group was armed with a gun.

Thank God, they hadn't seen him yet.

"Think about what you're doing," Serena pleaded.

Even Grant could see her words fell on deaf ears. The entire group took one menacing step closer.

"Traitor!" The leader in front shouted as he pointed the gun directly at Rico. "Rico Gonzales, you'll die a traitor!"

"No!" Serena shouted as she dove in front of Rico. The sound of a gunshot seared Grant's brain. Serena's body blocked Rico's for an endless moment, then jerked before hitting the ground.

"*Serena!*" Grant aimed and fired at the Hombres' leader, the one holding the gun. The rest of the kids scattered like rats, taking off in several directions. The shrill sound of police sirens filled the air. Grant could see that he'd hit his mark. The kid was lying motionless on the ground.

Ignoring him, Grant sprinted to Serena's side. Her limp form was also motionless and her blue scrubs were stained crimson.

"Oh, God, we need to call an ambulance." He pulled off his shirt and wadded it into a ball, then pressed it against the bloody hole in the left side of Serena's belly.

"I'll go." A strange voice spoke from behind him. Grant glanced around at one of the Hombres who hadn't left. He was about the same size and apparent age as Rico. By the meaningful glances the two boys exchanged, Grant figured the kid had once been Rico's friend. Maybe the one who had dragged him into the gang in the first place.

"My phone is in the rusty Chevy parked around

the bushes,'' he directed. The boy nodded and dashed off. The sounds of sirens grew louder.

Rico knelt on the grass on Serena's opposite side.

''Why did she do that?'' Rico whispered to Grant. ''She jumped right in front of me. Why?'' The boy's dark eyes were filled with guilty horror.

Grant was too choked up to answer. He knew Serena had risked her life for the boy out of love. She had the heart and soul of the very heroes she despised. But he couldn't worry about the reasons now. She was bleeding to death right in front of him. What could he do to save her life? The extent of his medical knowledge was only enough to cover the basics. He'd never felt so worthless in his entire life. He leaned his weight over the makeshift bandage, hoping to slow the bleeding.

Rico held onto Serena's hand, and glanced up again at Grant. ''I'm sorry,'' his voice was soft. ''This is my fault. First Marta, then Serena.'' He swallowed hard then dropped his gaze.

Grant pulled his attention away from Serena, using his knee for added pressure so he could lay his hand briefly on Rico's shoulder. ''None of this is your fault, Rico. The Hombres did this. That kid over there...'' he gestured to the body in the grass behind him ''...pulled the trigger, not you. Those kids attacked your sister. Don't be so hard on yourself. You were brave to stand up to them. You showed real courage to do what was right. At your age, I'm not so sure I would have had the guts to do the same thing.''

Rico straightened his shoulders, feeling better after hearing he'd acted with true bravery. Grant's stomach twisted in fear as he stared back down at Serena.

Her face was pale against the red-gold riot of curls that framed her features. Grant felt his heart lurch in his chest. God, he'd just found her again, after eighteen long months without her. He couldn't bear to lose her now.

''Be strong, Serena,'' his voice broke as he spoke to her, praying that somewhere deep inside she could hear him. ''Hang in there. Help is coming. Please, don't leave me, not like this.'' Where in the hell was that ambulance? He glanced at the road and relief hit when he saw the red and white lights coming closer. Finally. ''Help is almost here, sweetheart. I need you to be strong. To hang on.''

Along with the ambulance came the police. He wasn't surprised to see Captain Reichert show up. The guy didn't know when to quit. The Captain crossed over to check on the supine body of the boy he'd shot. ''This one is dead.''

''Well, Serena isn't.'' Grant didn't ease up his pressure on Serena's wound. He refused to even consider the possibility that she might not make it.

''Is someone going to tell me what the hell happened here?'' The captain glared at them, rubbing a hand over the center of his chest.

Grant ignored him. Luckily, before the captain could go off on another tirade, the paramedics arrived.

"What do we have here?"

"Gunshot wound to the abdomen." Grant didn't move as they surrounded Serena, hooking her up to their equipment.

"Heart rate 160 and tachy. Respirations shallow. She needs to be tubed."

"Go ahead, I'll start an IV."

"ET tube in place. Bilateral lung sounds. Pulse ox at 95 percent. She's looking better."

"I've already given a half-liter of fluid. BP still only 90 over 45."

The two men worked over Serena as Grant applied pressure on her wound. Once they'd gotten her as stable as they could manage, one of the men nudged Grant aside.

"Thanks, we'll take it from here."

Grant didn't want to leave Serena, but he moved out of their way. The monitor beeped with the reassuring sound of Serena's pulse. The sound echoed in his head. She was going to make it.

She had to.

The two paramedics worked over Serena in a synchronized harmony of movement. When they'd gotten a pressure dressing strapped over her abdominal wound, they lifted her onto the stretcher and wheeled her toward the waiting ambulance.

Grant tried to follow, but Captain Reichert grabbed his arm.

"Oh, no, you don't. I need some information and I mean now. Didn't I tell you to stay the hell away from my case?"

"Yeah, but…" Grant watched as the paramedics stowed Serena in the back of the ambulance. Rico came up to stand beside him, glancing at the captain uncertainly. Grant ground his teeth together in frustration. Obviously he couldn't leave this mess without some explanation. Once he'd satisfied the captain, he'd take Rico with him to the hospital. He couldn't leave the boy stranded here alone.

"Well?" The captain's irritated tone cut through his thoughts. "I'm waiting."

Grant glanced down at the scared boy at his side. "Rico? Why don't you start at the beginning?"

The story came out in bits and pieces but by the time they were finished, the captain appeared mollified. The body of the dead Hombre was photographed and taken away. The cops dispersed from the scene. Somehow they'd managed to round up and arrest a half-dozen of the Hombres thanks to information from Rico and his friend.

Grant wanted nothing more than to get over to Trinity Medical to see about Serena. When he turned back to the captain to ask if there was anything else he needed to do, he found the older man bent at the waist, his hands propped on his thighs just above his knees for support.

"Captain? You OK?"

"Yeah." But the word was faint, and Grant could hear the captain struggling to breathe.

"Hey, you'd better sit down." He guided the captain into the outbuilding and to one of the picnic tables located there.

"Damn." Ted continued to audibly gasp for breath. "I've had this nagging heartburn all day but now it feels like there's a damn elephant sitting on my chest."

"Maybe we'd better get you to the hospital." Grant wanted to go there anyway to see Serena, but he was genuinely worried about his boss. Even in the dim light he could see a fine sheen of sweat covering the captain's face. "No offense, sir, but you look like hell."

"I'll be fine after a few minutes. Just let me rest a minute."

Grant glanced around their dark surroundings. The park was fairly isolated and the officers had already left the scene. No way did he want the captain to stay here only to possibly grow worse.

"I don't think so." Grant turned to Rico. "Stay with him for a few minutes. I'll get my car and drive it over here. We're only a few miles from Trinity."

Rico nodded and Grant half loped to his car, favoring his injured thigh. He wondered if the captain was having a heart attack. He knew his boss had had heart trouble in the past. The car bumped and rattled over the grassy terrain as he drove right up to the outbuilding where the captain waited.

Within ten minutes he and Rico had gotten the captain into the back seat and over to Trinity Medical Center. Grant sent Rico inside to get someone out to help. In record time hospital personnel surrounded his car.

"What happened?" One young doctor crawled into the back seat, where Ted was slumped in the corner.

"He was having trouble breathing and complained it felt like an elephant was sitting on his chest."

"Does he have a history of heart problems?" The young doctor was backing out and gesturing for the gurney to be pulled up alongside the car.

"Yeah, he's had a heart attack in the past."

"Well, his classic symptoms tell me he's likely having another one now." The doctor and several nurses pulled the limp form of the captain out of the car and between them they shoved him onto the gurney.

Satisfied the captain was in good hands, Grant parked his car, then went in search of Serena. In the emergency department, he stopped at the front desk.

"Can you tell me the status of Serena Mitchell?"

"Are you a relative, sir?" The clerk used the computer to search for Serena's name.

"Yeah, I'm her fiancé." Hell, he wasn't exactly telling a lie. He fully intended for Serena to become his wife. The sooner, the better. Grant wasn't about to let minor details stand in the way of him being allowed in to see her.

"I'm sorry, but they've already taken her into the

operating room. You'll have to wait in the surgery waiting room. The doctor will call as soon as he's finished.''

''Surgery?'' Grant paled, though he shouldn't have been surprised.

''Yes. Does she have any other family that we should notify?'' The clerk frowned at her computer screen. ''I see she's an employee here, but the only person to call in case of an emergency is a Dana Whitney, another nurse who works here at Trinity.'' Now the clerk peered at him suspiciously over the top of her reading glasses. ''Are you sure you're her fiancé?''

Grant nodded. ''I swear. Our wedding is already planned for later this fall.'' And Serena would know that as soon as she awoke from surgery. He glanced down at a silent Rico. He'd almost forgotten about the kid. ''And how about Marta Gonzales? This boy here is her brother.''

''Hmm.'' The clerk entered the information then nodded. ''Yes, Marta Gonzales was admitted to a regular room. But it's too late for visitors.''

''Look, he just needs to know she's OK.'' Grant bit back a hiss of impatience. The security was tighter here than at the White House. These people were downright fanatical about their rules. ''I promise, five minutes and we're out of there.''

The woman let out a loud sigh. ''She's on the third floor general surgery unit. Room 315.''

''Thanks.'' Grant guided Rico by the shoulder toward the elevators. First he'd take the boy to see his sister, then he'd head back down to the waiting room.

Once upstairs on the third floor they found Marta's room without anyone seeing them. The nursing staff must have all been busy in other rooms. Easing open Marta's door, Rico ducked ahead of him into the darkened room.

"Marta?" The boy hesitantly approached the bed. Grant closed the door most of the way so only a sliver of light shone in. Hopefully, no one would notice their visiting violation.

"Rico?" From her position in the hospital bed, Marta held out a trembling hand. "I was so worried about you."

Rico ran to her side. "I'm sorry, Marta. So sorry."

"Shh." Marta smoothed a hand over his head. Her bruised face tilted in a lopsided smile. "I'm just glad to see you."

Rico sat in the chair next to Marta's bed and laid his head on the mattress beside her. Marta kept her hand on his head, stroking his hair.

Grant was glad to see Marta would be OK, but his feet shuffled nervously. What about Serena? He needed to get down to the waiting room so that he'd be there when the doctors came looking for him.

"Marta, I'm going to leave Rico here for a while." He hesitated to tell her about Serena being shot. The woman had enough to worry about right now without hearing that disturbing news. "I'll be back in a while."

"OK." Marta's eyes slid closed.

"Rico, stay put until I come back for you."

Rico nodded, looking as if he'd be content to spend the night if the hospital personnel would permit it.

Grant slipped from the room and headed back downstairs. He followed the signs and found the waiting room without difficulty. The area was deserted, but there was a small coffee-maker located in the corner of the room. Restless, he busied himself with making a pot of coffee.

Sipping the strong brew, Grant paced the length of the room, his stomach tied in knots. Half an hour later, a cute, petite, dark-haired nurse came into the waiting room wearing baggy blue scrubs. She halted abruptly when she saw Grant.

Slowly she approached him, sending him a tentative greeting. "Hi. I doubt you remember me, but I'm Dana, a good friend of Serena's."

"I remember." He frowned, then asked, "Have you heard anything about Serena's condition? Anything at all?"

"No. I happened to be working tonight when they called to tell me she'd been brought in. First I hear she left before the end of her shift, then I find out she was brought in after suffering a gunshot wound to the abdomen. Both are pretty untypical behavior for Serena. I don't suppose you know anything about what happened?"

Grant abruptly sat down in the nearest chair, dropping his head into his hands. "Cripes. Serena took off after Rico. I don't know why she didn't wait for me or simply call the police. She must have followed him to the park, facing the Hombres all by herself. I have no idea what she was thinking. There was no way she'd be able to talk them out of their insane gang mentality. They were determined to take out Rico, and they didn't give a damn who got in the way. The leader had a gun. He aimed at Rico but Serena jumped right in front of him, taking the bullet in her side." Grant dug his thumbs into his eye sockets, trying to erase the horrifying memory from his mind. "I should have been quicker to stop that stupid kid."

Dana sighed and dropped into the chair beside him. "Sounds like Serena is responsible for her own actions, not you. She is by far the most stubborn woman I know."

Grant couldn't forgive himself so easily. The vision of Serena's blood-stained blue scrubs haunted him. He finally understood why she hated his cop career. Watching someone you loved throw her life into the path of danger had been the most awful thing he'd ever seen. He'd lost years off his life. And the waiting was pure hell. He wished someone would tell him what was going on in that operating room.

"Hey, don't worry. We have the best trauma team in the state," Dana tried to reassure him. "Serena couldn't get better care anywhere else."

Grant nodded, but unconvincingly. "I know." He just couldn't stand the interminable waiting, wondering if Serena was going to pull through or not. What if he didn't get another chance?

Dana put a comforting hand on his arm, and reluctantly stood up. "I have to get back to work, I'm in the trauma intensive care unit tonight. I promise to call as soon as we hear any news." She regarded him thoughtfully. "Detective Sullivan, maybe you should get something to eat."

Grant dragged his hands over his face and shook his head. "No, I'll stay here." Dana poured him a fresh cup of coffee from the pot in the corner of the waiting room before heading back to work.

The waiting was killing him. Other people walked past the waiting room but he didn't pay any attention to them. All he could think about was Serena. She was desperately important to him. He remembered her touch, pulling him from the darkest bowels of hell after he'd been shot. He imagined her scent and the pure pleasure of making love with her. Hell, he could just sit across from her without saying a word and still be happy. He couldn't imagine a world without her. His heart physically ached at the thought of never being able to touch her or hold her again.

Finally a weary female doctor, wearing faded blue scrubs and looking far too young to be a surgeon, came into the waiting room. "Detective Grant Sullivan?"

Grant jumped up from his seat. "Yes? Is Serena going to be all right?"

The young doctor held out her hand and introduced

herself. "I'm Dr. Burns, I assisted the trauma team during the operation. Your fiancée suffered some serious internal bleeding, which took us a while to get under control. Luckily, the bullet missed most of her spleen, although we did repair a small laceration there, along with other various repairs of her small intestine. The angle was such that we were able to save her kidney. We're going to send her to the intensive care unit for the rest of the night because of the high risk of infection. Overall, her condition is serious but stable."

Grant closed his eyes for a moment, hardly daring to believe that Serena would survive. Then he pinned the tiny doctor with a hopeful look. "When can I see her?"

The woman shrugged, favoring him with a weary smile. "The nurses are getting her settled in now, they'll call you when you can come in. You can spend a little time with her, but then you should get some rest."

"Thank you." Grant watched as the young surgeon left the room.

True to her word, Dana came to get Grant about fifteen minutes later. "She's still out of it," Dana warned him. "She probably won't even know that you're there."

Grant didn't agree. Personal experience had taught him otherwise. "She'll know I'm there," he told Dana with heartfelt conviction. "Somehow, deep inside, she'll know."

The intensive care unit appeared very different from a visitor's point of view. There was a hustle and bustle of activity going on everywhere. The nurses were busy in their respective patients' rooms and he remembered how confidently Serena had moved through the routine of patient care. She dealt with the intimidating equipment like a pro. He stopped in the doorway to Serena's room, struck by how fragile she looked lying there beneath the monitoring equipment. Dana held his arm in a soothing gesture, quietly explaining everything to him.

Grant took a few tentative steps into the room, crossing over to the side of her bed. As if sensing his need for privacy, Dana left him alone.

Pulling up a chair, he sat as close to her as he could get, taking Serena's hand in his. When he began to speak, his voice sounded rusty from disuse.

"Serena, I'm here, and the doctors told me that you're going to be just fine." He bent his head, pressing his mouth to the back of her hand. The unfamiliar sensation of tears pricked his eyes.

"God, Serena, I was so scared. When you jumped out in front of Rico, my heart stopped. I thought for sure that punk had killed you." Grant swallowed hard. "I don't know how to tell you this, Serena, but I love you. And I'm scared, because I know you're the best thing to come into my life, but all I seem to do is cause you pain. Not just this physical pain, which is bad enough, but the emotional pain of being who I am and what I do for a living."

Grant didn't know if he was making any sense. Since Serena hadn't moved, he didn't think it mattered. From his own experience, the sound of a human voice was more important than the actual words. "Serena. I love you so much." And in that moment, Grant knew what he had to do.

Serena was the most important person in his life. His job was only that, a job. He'd already given eight years to the force, he could quit or transfer to something else.

He had to prove how much he loved her. He only prayed his decision wasn't too late.

CHAPTER THIRTEEN

THE nurses left him alone with Serena for nearly an hour. Grant didn't want to leave her side, but he still needed to fetch Rico. He was surprised the kid hadn't already been discovered. At any moment he expected Security to come looking for him, demanding he retrieve the boy.

Up on the third floor, he found Rico sleeping in the chair, his head still resting next to Marta. As he paused in the doorway, a nurse came up behind him.

"I wondered how that child got in here." She kept her voice low as to not wake them, but her eyes were full of disapproval. "He looks pretty young, no more than eleven or twelve. Don't you know he should be home in bed?"

"Yeah, but he lives with his sister who just happens to be the patient." Grant shrugged. "I don't think it's wise to let him stay home alone."

"Of course not." Horrified, she glared at him. "Isn't there anyone else he could stay with?"

Grant thought about Serena lying in the trauma ICU down the hall. She'd take the boy in a heartbeat. No matter how much he wanted to stay here close to Serena, he knew taking temporary custody of Rico was the right thing to do. Grant nodded. "Yeah, he can come home with me."

"I don't know." Now the nurse chewed her lip nervously. "Are you related to him? If you're not his guardian…"

"I'm a cop." At least, officially he was still a cop. The captain hadn't fired him, not yet anyway. The last time he'd checked, the captain had suffered another heart attack and was right now in the cardiac cath lab, having a procedure done to reopen the arteries in his heart. He fished his badge out of his pocket and presented it to the nurse. "Detective Sullivan, ma'am. Rico knows me. I promise he'll be safe."

The nurse pursed her lips then finally nodded. "I guess the boy can go home with you. Sheesh, I hope I don't get in trouble over this. I mean, how did I manage to get stuck with this problem? The kid wasn't even here when I started my shift." She plowed her fingers through her hair in a gesture of exasperation. "I hope you'll bring him back to see his sister tomorrow. Visiting hours start at eleven a.m."

"I will," Grant promised.

"Good. Now scat, before I change my mind."

Grant gently roused the boy. Rico blinked at him. "Huh?"

"We have to go home." He glanced at his watch. "It's almost two in the morning. We'll head back to my place to get some sleep. We can come back tomorrow.''

Rico frowned as if troubled by this news. ''I don't wanna go to your place. I wanna go home.''

Grant sighed. He could understand Rico's apprehension but what were his options? He didn't have a key to Serena's apartment, much less to Rico's.

''Rico knows how to get in,'' Marta whispered from the bed.

Grant raised his brow. He hadn't realized Marta was awake. He turned back to Rico. ''You do?''

''Yeah.'' The boy nodded earnestly.

''Let's go.'' Grant gestured to the door.

Rico gave his sister one last hug, then turned to go with Grant. They walked together through the eerily quiet hospital corridors. Grant thought about Serena, lying in the ICU, connected to seemingly endless wires and tubes.

He prayed that she would wake up soon. Now that he'd made his decision to change his career, he wanted to let her know. This time, he'd propose again completely understanding her very real fears.

How else would he convince her to give them another chance?

Serena gradually awoke to familiar sounds, although something wasn't quite right. Struggling to get the sleep from her eyes, she brought the room into focus.

She was in the hospital. Nothing so unusual about

that. Except that she was seeing the room from the wrong angle.

From the unhealthy side of a hospital bed.

Appalled, she grabbed the side rail and pulled herself upright. Her stomach muscles screamed in protest and she gasped. The monitor over her head triple-beeped in alarm. She was a patient? In the trauma ICU?

How had that happened?

Two nurses rushed in. ''Serena, what are you doing? You disconnected your monitor leads. You need to lie back and relax.''

''What happened?'' Serena's throat felt as if it were on fire. Dear God, if this was what Grant had gone through when he'd been shot, she hadn't given him nearly enough credit. Her stomach really *hurt*.

''You don't remember?'' The nurses exchanged worried glances.

Serena closed her eyes. The memories floated in. She'd chased after Rico. Asked the ED clerk to call Grant, then had gone straight to the park, looking for Rico.

Without trying to sneak up on them, she'd stumbled upon Rico, bravely facing a pack of Hombres all by his skinny self. At first she'd been angry, shouting at them.

Then she'd seen the gun. Raising her hands to show she hadn't been armed, she'd tried to reason with them. Tried to point out the reasons the Hombres should let them go.

But there had been no reasoning with the leader, who'd screamed at Rico, calling him a traitor. There had been no mistaking the crazed gleam in his eye. Maybe he'd been pumped up on drugs, she hadn't known for sure. All she'd known had been that he wouldn't hesitate to shoot Rico. She'd reacted instinctively, diving toward the boy. The sharp, blazing pain had robbed her of breath. She opened her eyes.

"I remember. The kid shot me. Is Rico all right?"

"I don't know who Rico is, but you were the only victim that I know of brought in from the scene. The trauma team performed surgery and the doctors were able to resect a portion of your small bowel and repair a spleen laceration. The angle of the shot was such that there was minimal damage. You were very lucky, Serena."

Funny, she didn't feel all that lucky. Every breath hurt and her throat felt like coarse sandpaper, but she forced herself to ask. "Grant?"

"Yeah, Dana mentioned something about your cop friend being here last night. But I called the waiting room when I got in and he wasn't there."

Serena closed her eyes. She vaguely remembered hearing his voice, telling her to hang on and begging her not to leave him like this. In her foggy dream, he'd told her that he loved her. Had he really meant it? She didn't know. Obviously, Grant wasn't here now. She wasn't sure if that was a good thing or a bad one. Either way, she felt like hell. Probably better he didn't see her like this.

"Water?"

"Ice chips," the nurse corrected. "You should know the routine by now."

She did but, good heavens, she wanted water in the worst way. She eyed the tiny medicine cup filled with ice chips. Would her nurse accept a bribe? Say twenty bucks for a glass of water? Doubtful, but worth a try.

"Here's the ice chips. You also need to do your coughing and deep-breathing exercises."

Serena did her best, trying to ignore the shaft of pain that stabbed her belly. Boy, the next time she made one of her patients cough and deep-breathe, she was going to be far more sympathetic. The exercises hurt like the dickens.

"Serena, Grant is here."

Her eyes widened in panic. "No, don't let him in."

"What?" Confused, the nurse stared at her. "I thought you just asked about him?"

She had, but now that she was more awake she knew she didn't want Grant seeing her like this. There was a tube in her nose that went down to her stomach and another tube in her bladder. Her hair was a tangled mess and she needed a toothbrush. She resembled the wicked witch of the west. No way did she want Grant to come in. Bad enough that the people she worked with on a regular basis had to see her like this.

"No. Just tell him I'm fine, but I don't want to see him." She rubbed a hand over her aching belly incision.

"If you're sure." The nurse regarded her doubtfully.

Serena took another ice chip, savoring the coolness against her parched throat. "I'm sure. Tell him I'll call him in a few days."

The nurse hurried away to do her bidding. Serena pushed away the wave of uncertainty that gripped her. Grant's feelings might be hurt, but in the end this was for the best. Grant was a fixer. He lived to solve problems, which was why he was such a great detective. Seeing her lying helpless in the hospital would only muddy the issues between them. He'd feel responsible for her. He'd give up his chance at a normal life with Loren and Ben if he thought she needed him.

Time to stop leaning on Grant, she admonished herself. Time to stand on her own two feet. Maybe she mourned the loss of having Grant beside her, but the practical side of her nature demanded that life get back to normal and as soon as possible.

She'd already cleaned out Daniel's room by herself, donating the items to a nearby women's shelter. Surely she could handle this.

When the team came to do rounds, Serena discovered they planned to send her out to a private room on the general surgical floor. She should have been relieved by the news that she must be getting better. But the hours dragged by slowly and she couldn't keep her thoughts from dwelling on Grant. Had he gone back to work? Was he angry or secretly relieved when she'd refused to let him visit?

After she'd been moved to a new room, Dana was her first visitor. Her friend greeted her with a cheerful hello, then frowning when she glanced around her room.

"Where's your bodyguard?" she wanted to know. When Serena gave her a blank look, Dana went on to elaborate. "Tall, broad-shouldered, sandy brown hair, handsome? You know, the cop?"

Neither one of them was prepared when Serena suddenly burst into tears at the innocent question. Dana's eyes widened in alarm, and she went to place a comforting arm around Serena's shoulders.

"Serena, what's wrong?" Dana couldn't hide her confusion.

"Nothing. Everything." Serena sniffled loudly as she tried to stem the flow of tears that streamed down her cheeks. "I told Grant to go away. I didn't want him to see me with all the wires and tubes." She sighed and blew her nose loudly, mindful of the soreness from the tube that had been removed an hour earlier. "I'm so confused, Dana. What if he's only here out of guilt?"

"Serena, for Pete's sake! He'd already seen you with all the wires and tubes. I watched that man hover over you last night. He stayed at your bedside talking to you until his voice was hoarse." Dana placed her hands on her hips, shaking her head in disgust. "Wake up, Serena. That guy is head over heels in love with you."

"He spoke to me last night after I was out of surgery?'' Serena stared at her friend in horror. She remembered Grant's voice but had thought that he'd only been with her in the park, not here in the hospital as well. ''Oh, my God, he saw me with a nasogastric tube hanging out of my nose? That's even worse than I thought. No wonder he feels sorry for me.''

Dana's lips twitched and she bit down hard on her lip to keep from laughing. The tactic didn't work, though, and a giggle escaped.

''That's not funny!'' Serena said defensively.

''Yes. Oh, yes, it is.'' Dana was now laughing so hard she had to hold onto the bed rail to keep from falling to the floor.

Serena was not amused. ''Dana, you're supposed to be my friend.''

''Serena, I am your friend,'' Dana chided gently. ''But you're not making any sense. The feelings between you and Grant aren't going to disappear for no reason. He's not going to be put off by a stupid tube. You saw him in worse shape after he was wounded, didn't you?''

Serena frowned. ''But that's different. I'm a nurse. I'm used to seeing things like that every day.''

''And he's a cop. I bet he sees much worse.'' The laughter faded from Dana's voice. ''Rena, you need to talk to him. You and Grant have been through a lot over these past few days. Important relationships don't come easy.''

Those were almost the same words Mrs. Eichstadt had used. Serena sighed. ''There's not much hope in rekindling our relationship. The other night, when I stared at that psycho kid with the gun, I really understood what Grant faces every day. Staying with me would destroy him. And if I let him leave his career for me, a part of his soul would shrivel up and die.'' She remembered the passion in his voice when he'd recounted the tale of his sister's disappearance. ''He needs to be a cop just as much as I need someone who will be there for me. There's nothing we can do to change the most elemental part of ourselves. Nothing will make this work.''

''Just talk to him,'' Dana begged. ''Be honest and talk to him. Tell him what you're feeling.''

Serena's shoulders slumped. ''Yes. You're right. I haven't always been honest with him. I never told him the truth about Daniel. But I have explained my feelings to him before. Somehow I need to be strong enough to let him go.''

''Should I call him for you?'' Dana laid her hand on the phone.

''No, they're going to take me to Radiology in a few minutes.'' Serena wasn't sure if she was grateful or resentful for the forced reprieve of facing Grant. Resigned, she lifted her chin. ''I'll call him when I get back.''

CHAPTER FOURTEEN

THE trip to Radiology for a chest X-ray was uneventful. Serena called Grant but there was no answer at his place. Instead of leaving a message, she decided to try again later. She closed her eyes and dozed until a knock at her door woke her up.

Struggling to sit, she called, "Come in."

Grant strode into her room, his expression serious. Rico came in beside him, glancing anxiously at her. Serena smoothed a hand over her hair, silently grateful she'd at least been able to take a shower earlier that day.

"Serena." Grant nodded in her direction. "Hope you don't mind, but Rico wanted to see you."

Rico wanted to see her? Why? Puzzled, she glanced between the two of them. "Uh, no, I don't mind. How are you, Rico?"

His brown eyes watched her anxiously and he took several steps toward her, then paused and thrust his hands into the front pockets of his pants.

"Come here, Rico." Serena flashed him a warm smile. "Don't I at least get a hug?"

He nodded and quickly rushed toward her. Serena reached over the edge of her hospital bed to envelop him in a huge hug. Rico's arms tightened spasmodi-

cally around her as he returned the gesture. She
sucked in a silent gasp when the sutures on her abdominal incision pulled.

"Why did you do it?" Rico asked in a low voice.
"Why did you jump out in front of me?"

Serena was momentarily taken aback by his question. She glanced over at Grant who still stood in the
doorway, as if unsure of his welcome. The expression
in his smoky gray eyes was enigmatic.

"I don't know," she admitted slowly. "I didn't
stop to think, Rico, I simply reacted. I couldn't stand
by and let him shoot you." Slowly, Serena realized
that her instinctive action was no different from what
Grant had done the night he'd been shot. No different,
for that matter, than what Eric had done the night he'd
died. Eric had gone into the burning house to save a
little girl's life. The decision to help someone at the
expense of your own safety was not a conscious one,
but rather a part of your nature.

Obviously, the "hero" gene had worked its way
into her DNA as well. She just hadn't ever put it to
the test until the night she'd faced the Hombres.

Surprised at the realization, Serena didn't know
what to say. Embarrassing how she'd carried such
anger at Grant for so long. Even if he wasn't a cop,
he would put his life on the line for another.
Especially a child. That was just part of who he was.
His career had nothing to do with him being a hero.
He could hand out parking tickets and still remain a
hero at heart.

Rico watched her anxiously, and Serena pushed her startling thoughts aside. "I'm glad I was able to help. You have another chance to think about how you want to live your life, Rico. Don't let it go to waste."

"I have no words to thank you." His eyes were suspiciously bright. "Most of the Hombres were arrested. Others want nothing more to do with them. I think we're finally safe."

"No thanks are necessary." Serena swallowed hard and reached for his hands to give them a brief squeeze. "You can thank me by taking care of Marta. How is she?"

Rico shrugged his thin shoulders. "She's OK. She's in the hospital, too, but they're going to let her go today."

Serena grimaced. Marta had been kept in the hospital overnight? What about Rico?

"I hope you stayed home last night." Serena worried her lower lip between her teeth. Hopefully the social worker wouldn't need to know that Rico had been without parental supervision for the past twenty-four hours.

"He did. I stayed at his place with him." Grant spoke up from the doorway.

"Thank you, Grant."

He shrugged negligently. "No problem. Rico, we need to get moving. We still need to get Marta home before the game."

"Game?" Confused, Serena glanced between the

two of them. Grant had just gotten there but he was planning to leave already? "What game?"

"A T-ball game." Rico turned to Grant with a puzzled expression. "What's the boy's name? Ben?"

Grant cleared his throat and nodded. "Yeah, Ben. I promised Ben I'd come watch his game tonight. Rico is coming with me. We thought we'd stop and see if there is a summer league Rico can still join."

"Oh. That's great." Serena knew her flat tone betrayed her less than enthusiastic response. "Have fun. Tell Marta I'm glad she's on the mend."

"I will." Rico leaned over to give her one last hug. "Thanks, Serena. Hope you come home soon."

"Me, too." She stared at Grant who hadn't ventured more than a few steps into her room. The distance between them could have been miles instead of feet. Had she dreamed those whispered words? Had they been nothing more than wishful thinking? "Goodbye, Rico. Grant."

They left and the door of her room closed loudly behind them. Serena fought a fresh wave of useless tears. She'd let Grant go eighteen months ago, without realizing how ridiculous her demands had been. And now that she'd finally realized the truth, it was eighteen months too late.

Grant might still care about her—the night they'd spent together was proof they were very much physically compatible. But he didn't need her.

Not in the same way she needed him.

*   *   *

After taking Marta and Rico home, Grant stayed long enough to make sure the two had everything they needed. His mind, though, was back in the hospital with Serena.

She hadn't wanted to see him, that much was clear. What he didn't understand was why. The frozen expression in her eyes when Rico had mentioned Ben's T-ball game hadn't made sense. Certainly she couldn't think he still had something going with Loren? Not when he'd told her there was nothing but friendship between them? And especially not after they'd made love?

But she'd also sent him away when he'd come to visit. The nurse had been apologetic but very clear on that.

Marta seemed grateful that Grant was taking Rico out for a while. The poor girl still looked horrible with the dark bruises marring her pretty face. Grant itched to finish what Rico had started by going after the rest of the Hombres, intent on making them pay for what they'd done.

Ben was thrilled that he showed up at the game and chattered non-stop after he'd hit a double. Loren had kept her distance, as if knowing Grant was really only there for Ben.

Grant felt bad for Loren but he wasn't in charge of her happiness. She needed to figure that out on her own. Rico was able to join a team of twelve-year-olds, and when Grant dropped him off at home he talked more than usual, asking endless questions about baseball rules.

Glancing at his watch, Grant realized that there was still an hour before the end of hospital visiting time. With a sigh he turned his rusted Chevy toward home. Maybe Serena needed time to come to grips with her close call. She'd certainly seemed startled when Rico had asked why she'd jumped in front of him. Hell, Grant himself had lost years off his life when she'd pulled that stunt.

He didn't sleep well that night, his thoughts tumbling around in his head. Had Serena changed her mind about him? Would she give him a chance to make things right? The next morning, he couldn't stand the questions another minute and decided he would confront Serena once and for all.

At Trinity, he belatedly remembered the captain. Asking for Ted Reichert's room, he discovered his boss had been transferred out of the cardiac ICU the previous day.

"Captain." Grant grinned at the scowl etched in his boss's features. "I see you're doing better."

"Hmph." The captain didn't seem too happy to see him either. What was with everyone? Why was he suddenly *persona non grata* around here? "Sullivan. You're lucky I'm stuck in this hospital or I'd be putting a discipline in your file."

"Yeah, yeah." Grant shrugged off the threat. "Seriously, Captain, how are you? Did the doctors fix your heart?"

"Not really. They opened one artery but it turns out I have several that have become blocked again. They're talking about open-heart surgery. I'm already scheduled for tomorrow."

Grant drew a deep breath. "Wow, Captain, I'm sorry. I had no idea you needed surgery."

"Me neither." Glum, the captain glared at him. "I bet you're happy, though."

"What do you mean?"

"I'm officially retiring. And you're next in line for promotion."

Grant wasn't sure if the captain was serious or not. "Look, Captain, there's no need to make any rash decisions. Why don't you wait until after your surgery to decide whether or not to retire? Heck, let the department pay your medical leave."

"Ha!" The captain barked out a laugh. "Good one, Sullivan. I probably will do just that, but I've already made my decision. Hell, this is my second surgery. The docs have told me to turn my life around or face dying in the next five years. Make no mistake, I'm going to retire." He eyed Grant with a raised brow. "And I'm telling you, Sullivan, the job is yours if you want it."

Speechless, Grant didn't know what to say. Even more, he wondered what Serena would say. Would a leadership role make her happier than having him on the front line? "I'll think about it, Captain. I promise you, I'll seriously consider the promotion."

Grant headed down to the third-floor surgical unit,

the same floor where he'd been a patient not that long ago. Serena's door was open, and when he glanced in he was surprised to find her dressed in a fresh pair of scrubs, no doubt donated by the hospital. He couldn't imagine her blood-stained ones were salvageable.

"Serena." He tucked his hands into the front pockets of his jeans. "Are you getting ready to leave?"

"Oh, Grant." She swung around to face him then winced and placed a hand on her side. "I wasn't expecting you."

"Need a ride?"

"Well, actually, that would be great. I was going to call a cab."

He tamped down a flare of irritation. "You could have called me, you know."

She dropped her gaze. "Yes," she admitted softly. "I know."

What in the hell was going on with her? They needed to talk, but not here. First he'd get her home.

"It was nice of you to come," Serena added.

"Nice?" Grant took a few steps toward her, his fingers itching to pull her into his arms and let actions speak for him. He wasn't always good with words. "Is that why you think I'm here, Serena, because I'm nice?"

Serena shrugged helplessly. "I don't know, Grant. Everything is so confusing right now."

He wasn't confused, he knew exactly what he wanted. Serena. In his life. Permanently. But he chose

not to point that fact out. Instead, he waved a hand
at her small bag of personal items on the bed. "Is
that everything? Do you have any paperwork you
need to sign?"

Just then Dr. Burns walked into the room. "Your
X-rays look great, Serena, so you're free to go. I'll
give you prescriptions for antibiotics and pain medicine, and don't forget, I want to see you back in the
clinic in a few days."

Serena nodded and Grant knew that she was more
familiar with the routine than most. When Serena was
ready to leave, he met her out front, wishing he'd
brought his newer car rather than this beat-up old
Chevy.

He helped her in, reaching over to pull the seat belt
carefully over her abdominal incision. As Grant
pulled away from the curb, she turned toward him.

"I can't believe you still own this car. How many
miles are you up to? Two hundred thousand?"

He shot her a narrowed look. "Yes, if you must
know, I just broke that milestone. But I do have another car. If I had known that you needed a ride, I
would have brought that one instead."

"I don't need special treatment, Grant." Serena
leaned back in her seat.

"Yes, you do." And Grant vowed to find a way to
explain that to her once they reached her apartment.

At her place, he helped her with a supporting arm
under her elbow as she mounted the stairs. In her

apartment, she shuffled to the sofa and sank down gratefully.

"Thanks for bringing me home, Grant." She smiled at him, but it was a sad smile. His gut tightened anxiously.

"Serena, we need to talk." He dropped her bag on the floor, then sank into a chair beside her.

She nodded. "We do need to talk. I have to be honest with you, Grant. I realized something about heroes the other night."

"You know what I think a hero is?" Grant interrupted. "A hero is someone who faces illness and death every day, but who goes on enjoying life anyway. A hero is someone who suffers a devastating personal loss but who manages to give her gift of love, despite her grief. You're a hero, Serena, and not just because of how you saved Rico's life. Because of what you do every day."

"I…" She stared at him in surprise. "I think that's the nicest thing anyone has ever said to me."

"I love you, Serena. I also discovered something the other night. I finally understand the fear you've lived with since Eric died. I'm willing to give up my job for something less dangerous."

"Grant, I—"

He held up a hand. "Wait, let me finish. The night you were shot, the captain suffered a heart attack. I went to see him before I came to your room. He told me he's going to retire. He also thinks I'm in line to take his position. I'd be managing people and cases instead of arresting crooks." Grant almost smiled at Serena's shocked expression and he held her gaze with his. "I'll take the position if you'll give us another chance, Serena."

"Grant, you don't have to take the job, unless you want to."

"I don't?" He fought a flash of panic. Did that mean she would give him another chance or not?

Serena reached across the space between them to place a hand on his arm. "Grant, I want you to be happy. I love you. I was so stupid to ever let you go. No matter what you choose to do, I promise I'll support you."

A slow grin spread across his features. Grant stood and pulled Serena into his arms for a gentle embrace. "Are you sure, Serena? I love you too much to risk losing you again."

Serena nodded. "I'm sure. You're a hero, Grant, no matter what you choose to do. I know that now."

"Thank God, sweetheart. Because I love you so much that it scares me to death." Grant's words were muffled against her hair. "I love you." The words were easier to say the second time. "I want you to know, if they offer it to me, I plan on accepting the promotion. Not just for you, but for both of us and the family I hope we have one day." Grant captured her hand in his and slipped a familiar ring on the third finger of her left hand. Her original emerald engagement ring. He'd kept it these past eighteen months.

Tears filled Serena's eyes as she threw herself back into his embrace.

"Will you marry me?" Grant could barely get the question out. She was squeezing him so tight, he figured she had to be hurting her incision. "Will you marry me and be the mother of my children?"

"Yes," Serena whispered into his ear as she lifted her face to smile tearfully at Grant. Her hero. Her husband-to-be. "A thousand times, yes."

Grant buried his face in her hair, holding her with heartfelt relief. His heroine. Soon to be his wife.

He kissed her and held her gently, sure in the knowledge that together their love was strong enough to survive anything the future had in store for them.

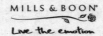

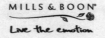

1204/024/MB110

Christmas is a time for miracles...

Christmas Deliveries

Caroline Anderson   Marion Lennox

Sarah Morgan

On sale 3rd December 2004

Available at most branches of WHSmith, Tesco, ASDA, Martins, Borders, Eason, Sainsbury's and all good paperback bookshops.

...Michelle Reid...
.....Jane Porter
Susan Stephens....

One
Christmas
Night

On sale 3rd December 2004

Available at most branches of WHSmith, Tesco, ASDA, Martins,
Borders, Eason, Sainsbury's and all good paperback bookshops.

4 FREE

BOOKS AND A SURPRISE GIFT!

We would like to take this opportunity to thank you for reading this Mills & Boon® book by offering you the chance to take FOUR more specially selected titles from the Medical Romance™ series absolutely FREE! We're also making this offer to introduce you to the benefits of the Reader Service™—

- ★ FREE home delivery
- ★ FREE gifts and competitions
- ★ FREE monthly Newsletter
- ★ Exclusive Reader Service offers
- ★ Books available before they're in the shops

Accepting these FREE books and gift places you under no obligation to buy, you may cancel at any time, even after receiving your free shipment. Simply complete your details below and return the entire page to the address below. You don't even need a stamp!

YES! Please send me 4 free Medical Romance books and a surprise gift. I understand that unless you hear from me, I will receive 6 superb new titles every month for just £2.69 each, postage and packing free. I am under no obligation to purchase any books and may cancel my subscription at any time. The free books and gift will be mine to keep in any case.

M4ZED

Ms/Mrs/Miss/Mr ....Initials ....
BLOCK CAPITALS PLEASE

Surname ....

Address ....

....

....Postcode................................

Send this whole page to:
UK: FREEPOST CN81, Croydon, CR9 3WZ